Ghost Town

Riding into unknown territory, Clint Shane and his pal Ty Morrow think they have found a settlement where they can rest and buy fresh provisions. The amiable youngsters are in a good mood as they ride towards the sprawling town when suddenly shots ring out.

Terrified they spur their mounts and gallop across the wild terrain towards the array of buildings which are bathed in blinding sunlight. As they reach the outlying structures a chilling realization dawns on the pair: this is no ordinary town; there are no people.

As they hastily dismount, the drifters notice that every building is crumbling beneath the merciless rays of the sun. As more shots ring out, Morrow and Shane realize they have taken refuge in a Ghost Town.

Ghost Town

Roy Patterson

A Black Horse Western

ROBERT HALE · LONDON

ISBN 978-0-7198-1494-5

Robert Hale Limited
Clerkenwell House
Clerkenwell Green
London EC1R 0HT

www.halebooks.com

Typeset by
Derek Doyle & Associates, Shaw Heath
Printed and bound in Great Britain by
CPI Antony Rowe, Chippenham and Eastbourne

Dedicated to my friends
Karl, Raye and Ross

PROLOGUE

The vast lands that have become known by the collective name of the Wild West have many faces. Nothing that is known in the gentler terrains found on the eastern seaboard could ever prepare anyone for what lies beyond the notorious Pecos. Rivers of acid flowing between poisonous plants of the most delicate hues can deceive even the most experienced of souls. Nothing can be trusted or taken for granted.

Innocently to do so was to dance with death.

The bleached bones of the unwary were strewn along the trails used by the first wagon trains. The land could go from desert to ice-cold forest within only a few hours.

Men died just for misjudging what they rode into.

The West took no prisoners.

It had a million ways of killing the naive. It had no mercy and punished the ill-prepared or those who simply ignored its warnings.

A simple journey from one town to another could prove deadly to those who did not understand the simple truths of the terrain's total power over mere humans.

For countless centuries men thought that they had the power to subdue nature. Men have built many a magnificent edifice in a vain attempt to conquer the unconquerable, and have seen them destroyed in only seconds by angry storms. Some of their largest ships have sunk without trace when they have challenged the sea. Nothing man has ever created can equal the might of nature when its dander is up.

Two young men riding through a terrain of varying climates found to their cost that it did not pay to take anything for granted.

The blistering heat alternating with wintry cold should have warned them that they were heading into a place like no other. This was an unholy land.

One in which to be wary.

The vast land known simply as the Wild West

had a million ways to kill the innocent. The two young men in search of a distant town and jobs as lawmen found to their cost that it did not pay to enter some terrains uninvited.

Even in a land of unimaginable horrors there were often men who were as deadly and unforgiving as the terrain itself.

These were creatures who were shunned by civilization and exiled to roam the wastelands in search of their next unsuspecting prey. Some said they were the imaginings of minds tortured by the hostile climate but, whatever the truth, they were real to those who encountered them.

No imaginings ever fired deadly guns.

The two young riders had ridden west believing the land they were journeying across was the same as the one they had left far behind them.

Soon they would discover they were wrong.

Soon their only hope was that whatever gods dwelled in this strange and inhospitable land might deem it fit to look kindly upon them.

But there are some places that have not been created by merciful gods.

The innocent riders had meant no harm, yet their ignorance of this strange territory into which they had entered had caused untold dangers to be unleashed upon them.

As always, it was not just the hostile terrain that posed great danger to the riders. There were other things to be cautious of: venomous sidewinders shared the desert upon which they had ventured, as did gun-toting men who called these places home.

The two young horsemen were searching for a settlement called Arapaho Springs.

What they found was a town as dead as the poor souls who had once inhabited it.

A ghost town.

ONE

The land was a mix of torrid, sun-bleached terrain flanked by vast forested ice-capped mountains. Where the trees ended the deadly prairie began. There seemed no sense to it to the pair of horsemen who steered their mounts down from the icy wastes into the blistering heat. Neither Clint Shane nor his best pal Ty Morrow had ever experienced anything like this unholy land as they urged their horses down on to the level ground and faced the vast stretch of prairie.

Shane dragged his reins back and stopped his buckskin mount. Morrow slowed his own horse and drew leather as he reached his partner. They stood in their stirrups and surveyed the desolate prospect. Both men looked at one another and shook their heads in confusion.

'What in tarnation have we ridden into, Clint?' Morrow queried. 'How many seasons are we gonna ride through?'

'You're right, Ty,' Clint said, mopping his brow on his shirtsleeve. 'We sure have ridden through all four seasons since sunup, and it ain't even noon yet.'

'I don't get it.' Morrow sighed. 'I've put my coat on and taken it off so many damn times I'm getting plumb giddy.'

Shane smiled and reached across to pat his partner on the back.

'Leastways, we are still headed west by my reckoning.'

Morrow looked all around the landscape. The hot sand was pristine and unmarked. Not one animal had moved across it for a while. A few cacti stood at intervals ahead of them, looking like wounded men with their arms raised. The sun was high and burned through their trail gear as Morrow lifted himself off his saddle and slowly dismounted.

'Why you getting down from that white-faced nag, Ty?' Shane asked. 'We still got us a lot of ground to cover if'n we're to reach Arapaho Springs.'

Morrow rested his gloved hands on the top of his saddle and looked across it at his friend.

'Don't you figure these horses deserve a drink, Clint?' he asked.

Shane shrugged and dismounted. 'I guess they do. I'm so damn confused by this damned terrain I'm all mixed up.'

Morrow pulled his canteen from his saddle horn and unscrewed its stopper. He sighed and then removed his black Stetson.

'I don't know where we are but wherever it is I'm sure spooked by it,' he admitted. He dropped his hat on the sand and poured some water into it. He watched as his horse dropped its head and started drinking.

Shane removed his own hat and dropped it on to the sand. He reached for his canteen.

'I know what you're saying, Ty,' he answered. 'This land just don't fit no pattern that I've ever heard tell about. How can we keep going from snow to sand in a few hours? It just don't make no sense. No sense at all.'

Morrow replaced his canteen. 'It was your idea to head this way, as I recall.'

Shane poured water into his upturned hat bowl and screwed the stopper back on the canteen.

'The paper was advertising the jobs, Ty,' he said with a smile. 'I just noticed it.'

'And you said you'd found us a real easy couple of jobs and all we had to do was head west.' Morrow smiled too. He pulled out his tobacco pouch and started to roll himself a smoke. 'Arapaho Springs need themselves two experienced law officers. Perfect for us, you said.'

'It is perfect for us.' Shane nodded. 'The salary is twice what we was earning as deputies back in Salt Flats.'

'The weather was a damn sight less ornery back there though,' Shane pointed out.

They stepped into their stirrups and pulled themselves up on to their saddles. The two men tapped their spurs against the sides of the two horses and steered them forward. The horses were as exhausted by the constant changes in temperature as their masters, but they obeyed and moved on into the blistering heat haze.

Morrow moved himself ahead of his partner and lifted himself up again. He balanced in his leather stirrups and focused as far as the shimmering air would allow.

'You see anything, Ty?' Shane asked. He had

14

slumped over the horn of his saddle and was teasing his long leathers to keep his mount moving.

Morrow turned his head and stared at his pal.

'I can't see a damn thing,' Morrow answered. 'Are you sure we're headed west, Clint?'

Shane pulled out what looked like a pocket watch and flipped its silver lid. His red-raw eyes looked down into the palm of his hand at the compass. He nodded his head.

'We're headed west OK, Ty.'

Morrow sat back down upon his saddle, lifted his head and glared at the scenery, which was becoming oppressive.

'We're gonna reach another damn mountain range by the looks of it.' Morrow sighed and shook his head. 'I'm getting kinda sick of this.'

Without uttering another word Shane tapped his spurs and drew level with his partner. He slipped the compass into his vest pocket, then reached out and gave Morrow's shirtsleeve a gentle tug. Morrow glanced quickly at Shane.

'What?'

Shane did not explain. He was staring far to their left. Morrow swung himself around to follow his companion's gaze.

The answer became swiftly apparent.

Both riders drew rein and stopped their mounts again.

'You see them?' Shane whispered as if his words might be overheard.

Morrow gave a slow nod of his head.

'Yep, I see them sure enough,' he replied drily.

'Who do you figure they are, Ty?' Shane wondered.

Morrow held his horse in check. His narrowed eyes were glued to the four riders moving high along the brow of a high dune. They were a few hundred feet away, but both Shane and Morrow felt vulnerable.

The four horsemen had spotted them a long time previously. They had kept pace with the two lost souls.

'Who are they, Ty?' Shane pressed his pal for an answer he knew would never come.

Morrow dragged his horse round until it faced the quartet of riders. He studied them, puzzled.

'They look like they're tracking us, Clint,' Morrow said at last, glancing back at Shane. 'They were trailing our every move. They were riding on the rim of that dune and then stopped when we stopped.'

'What does that mean?' Shane asked. He rested one hand upon his holstered gun grip whilst with the other he held his reins up to his chest. 'Who'd be tracking our sorrowful hides out here in the middle of nowhere?'

Morrow backed his horse up to his partner's. He bit his lip and sighed deeply.

'That's the question that's troubling me, Clint,' he admitted. His free hand curled its fingers around his holstered gun.

'Who do you figure they are?'

Morrow continued to stare up through the warm air that shimmered between themselves and their observers.

'If I knew that I'd be a lot less nervous,' he replied. He looked all around them for cover. There was no cover, only sand and the occasional cactus.

'Can you make them out?' Shane asked.

'Nope, they're too far away and they got the sun on their backs,' Morrow said. 'They could be anyone. The only thing I can tell for sure is that they're riding horses.'

Clint Shane swallowed hard. 'I got me a feeling they might be bandits, Ty. This sure looks like the kinda place where bandits would hide out.'

Morrow summoned every scrap of his dwindling strength and swung his horse to face directly ahead once again.

'They could be Injuns,' he remarked. 'They might just be curious.'

'Do you reckon?' Shane steadied his mount.

Morrow raised an eyebrow. 'Let's keep these nags walking and see what them critters do.'

Both riders tapped their spurs and urged their mounts to continue their long journey through the soft white sand towards the distant trees.

The horses obeyed and trotted at a slow pace through the hot desert. With each stride both Shane and Morrow watched as the four horsemen kept pace with them along the crest of the sand dune.

'They're sticking with us, Ty,' Shane hissed through gritted teeth. 'Them bastards are matching us stride for damn stride.'

Morrow gripped his reins in his gloved hand and stared through the shimmering air at the four riders. For more than a mile they all rode west. The terrain was growing even more parched.

Then something appeared far ahead of them.

Shane kept his mount level with his partner's

horse and screwed up his eyes. He could see something but, through the heat haze, he was not sure what it was.

'What is that?' He pointed straight ahead.

'I ain't sure, Clint,' Morrow replied.

The dancing shapes slowly became clearer, taking form as the pair of horsemen came closer to them.

'That's a town!' Morrow shouted out gleefully. 'We damn found Arapaho Springs, buddy. We found it.'

Shane gave out a loud hoot, then laughed in a mixture of happiness and relief.

'Thank the Lord!' Shane yelled. 'We found the damn town without even knowing we was close.'

Morrow looked over his shoulder. His smile vanished from his face. It was replaced by a look of total disbelief.

'They're gone.'

Shane too looked to the dunes. His smile also faded.

As they continued to urge their mounts on to the distant town both riders now had two questions burning into their skulls.

Who were the four riders who had followed them and where had they gone?

Morrow lifted his long leathers and whipped the shoulders of his horse. His panic was only matched by Shane's as he spurred his mount.

Both horsemen thundered towards the strange apparition that they prayed might prove to be their salvation.

TWO

Every sinew in the two horsemen's bodies was
screaming for them to find refuge from the
threat they both sensed. The exhausted horses
faithfully obeyed their masters and churned up
the soft sand as they galloped towards the distant
buildings. Yet the town seemed to get no closer,
no matter how desperately the two riders spurred
their horses. Both mounts leapt like pumas
across a massive sinkhole as the riders balanced
like tightrope walkers in their stirrups. Their
intrepid flight seemed to last an eternity to both
the young riders as they drove their mounts up
over a sandy rise, then dropped down upon the
remnants of what had once been a well-travelled
road.

With each long stride of their mounts they expected to hear the devilish sound of gunfire and feel the bullets of the mysterious four horsemen they had spied a couple of miles behind them.

But nothing apart from the sound of their horses' hoofs filled their ears. Morrow and Shane dared not look behind them for fear that even a glance might bring lethal lead homing in upon their exposed backs.

Both horses were drained of strength by the relentless sun, which bore down upon them and every other living creature in the desert, but they obediently found a pace which kept them heading towards their riders' goal. Then Morrow and Shane, to their utter surprise, saw something neither of them had expected. They stared ahead in disbelief as they drew closer and closer to the scattered buildings.

It was obvious that here had once been a living town, like so many others still to be found across the territory. But it was now little more than a crumbling memory.

Morrow leaned back against his cantle and stared at the town towards which their mounts were galloping. He glanced across at his partner, who looked equally bewildered by the unexpected sight.

Both riders slowed their horses as they reached the outskirts of the town, then stopped. Morrow shook his head as their hoof dust overtook them.

Every building was the colour of sand. Every drop of moisture had been sucked from its heart by the merciless sun which blazed down upon them. Morrow turned his mount and looked at each of the weathered buildings. He had heard tales of such places but had never imagined that one day he would ride into one of them.

'What the hell have we ridden into, Ty?' Shane asked his friend. 'Where are all the folks?'

Morrow tried to find an answer but his mind kept dwelling upon the fact that only moments earlier he had wrongly thought they had found their salvation in the heart of the untamed land. They had both thought that they would be safe once they mingled among the townsfolk.

There was always safety in a crowd but now, Morrow realized, they were exposed and alone.

The bewildered Shane urged his mount forward and dismounted beside a dried water trough. The horse dropped its head and snorted.

Shane turned to his still silent partner.

'There ain't no water in this trough, Ty,' he gasped.

Morrow turned his attention to his pal and also dismounted. He led his lathered-up mount towards the wooden trough. His eyes looked into it.

'There's plenty of sand, Clint,' he commented.

'This ain't funny, Ty,' Shane shouted.

Morrow nodded. 'I know.'

Clint Shane looked heavenwards in despair. 'What kinda place is this?'

'This is what they call a ghost town, Clint,' Morrow said, rubbing his throat. 'First one I've ever seen.'

Shane rested his weight on the trough and stared around them. Every building looked as though it were ready to collapse. He could not comprehend how such a place could be built and then abandoned.

'You mean that every damn man, woman and kid has left this town, Ty?' he asked. 'How can an entire town's population just up and leave?'

Morrow checked the water pump beside the trough. It looked as dry as the town's buildings.

'I figure I might be able to prime this pump,'

he said.

Shane did not hear his friend's words. He just looked at Morrow. 'Are you telling me that all the people who used to live here just left, Ty?'

Morrow pulled his canteen from the saddle and unscrewed its stopper. He shook it and knew that there was enough liquid inside it for what he intended to do.

'Yep. That's what they did, Clint.' Morrow nodded as he moved closer to the pump. 'They just up and left.'

Shane watched as his pal primed the pump and started to crank its long metal arm.

'Where in tarnation would they go, Ty?' He stood and moved around their horses as Morrow continued to crank the pump's lever. 'I wonder why they left?'

Suddenly a few droplets of water dripped from the pump. A few heartbeats later water poured into the trough.

Morrow kept pumping as he stared at his partner.

'Well, one thing's for sure, Clint,' he stated. 'It weren't coz they were out of water. There's plenty of the stuff down below. I reckon there's an underground reservoir, which is fed from the

25

snow-capped mountains.'

Shane moved to the trough and stared at the crystal-clear liquid as it flowed from the metal mouth of the pump into the trough.

'So they had plenty of water, huh?'

'Yep, they had plenty of water.' Morrow stopped cranking the lever and rested. The rays of the sun danced across the surface of the water. He removed his gloves and scooped up enough to drink. He drank from the cupped palms of his hands, then gave out a satisfied sigh. 'Mighty sweet water, Clint. Taste it.'

Shane forced himself between the two thirsty horses and emulated his pal. The water felt good as it made its way down his throat.

'Where'd you learn how to prime a water pump?' Shane asked, wiping his mouth across his shirtsleeve. 'I never knew that was what you had to do to them to make them work.'

Morrow smiled and moved away from the trough.

'I thought even the dumbest of critters knew how to get a pump working,' he answered wryly.

'Reckon my education must have missed that lesson,' Shane said. He looked at Morrow, who was now standing beyond their drinking mounts.

He paced towards his thoughtful pal. 'What's eating at you, Ty?'

Morrow's eyes were scanning the surrounding sand dunes, which towered over the ghost town.

'Have you forgotten the four riders who were dogging our trail, Clint?' Morrow asked as his eyes searched the sand dunes for a hint of them. 'They were trailing our every move and then all of a sudden they disappeared. Where'd they go?'

Shane removed his hat and beat the desert from it against his pants leg. He replaced the Stetson on his head and bit his lower lip anxiously.

'I'm wondering who they are.'

Ty Morrow looked at his friend. 'Yeah, that's bin troubling me too. Who were those riders?'

'And why didn't they kill us when they had the chance?' Shane added. 'They might be just lost like we are, but that don't sit well with me.'

'Me neither,' Morrow admitted. Then he turned on his heel and looked at the adobe buildings again.

The weathered buildings of the ghost town had once been painted up like those in all of the other towns they had visited. This place was different. The blazing sun had burned every scrap of paint from all the buildings and Morrow knew that that took time. An awful lot of time.

'How long do you figure this town has been abandoned, Ty?' Shane asked, diverting his attention from the surrounding desert to his pal.

'Years,' Morrow replied with a sigh. 'A town don't just dry out like this 'un has in a few months. Nope, by my reckoning this town was abandoned years ago.'

'How'd you figure that?'

'Look at it.' Morrow pointed at the various buildings. 'Paint don't peel off like that in a few months, Clint. This place has been dying for years.'

Suddenly both their horses raised their heads from the trough and pricked their ears. Morrow patted his pal's shoulder and aimed his gun finger at the disturbed horses.

'They've heard something, Clint.'

Shane drew his gun and turned on the heels of his boots, looking hard as he tried to discover what had alarmed their trusty mounts.

'I don't see nothing, Ty,' he said, moving back to their alerted horses. 'What you figure it was that spooked our nags?'

Before Morrow had a chance to reply a shot

rang out in the distance. Both men instinctively ducked as the bullet cut through the dry air.

The deafening noise echoed off the sun-bleached buildings like a clap of thunder. Both horses backed away from the trough. One reared up and gave out a whinny.

Then another equally loud shot rocked the street. A bullet cut through the dry air and took a chunk from the rim of the trough. Splinters erupted under the heads of the already skittish horses as burning debris showered over the animals.

Both their horses shied away from the trough in total terror.

'The horses!' Morrow shouted as he realized what their mounts were about to do. 'Quick, Clint. They're gonna high-tail it.'

Morrow and Shane raced towards them but there was no way of stopping frightened horse-flesh in full flight. Morrow grabbed at the bridle of his mount but the powerful animal threw him aside as if he were a fly its tail was swatting.

Morrow rolled over and stared through the dust at the two horses galloping away in fright. He scrambled back to his feet, his gaze following in horror as, panicked, they bolted and headed for the desert.

'Damn it all!' he cursed.

Realizing that it was pointless even attempting to chase their fleeing horses, Shane stopped in his tracks and turned back to Morrow.

'Who the hell's shooting at us, Ty?' he asked.

Another shot echoed around the dilapidated buildings. A plume of dust rose up between the two men as the bullet buried itself into the ground.

The quick-witted Morrow ran across the churned-up sand, grabbed his pal by the shoulder and dragged him towards the nearest building. Morrow released his grip when they were under the cover of the nearest porch overhang.

They had barely reached the termite-riddled upright when another two blasts carved through the dry air and hit the corner of the wall.

Morrow screwed up his eyes.

'Where in tarnation are they?' he snarled. 'I can't see anyone firing a gun.'

'Me neither,' Shane agreed. 'It's like we was being shot at by ghosts.'

'It sure ain't ghosts, Clint,' Morrow said, vainly holding his six-shooter, waiting for a target to aim at. 'The only thing I know for sure is that it ain't ghosts.'

Two more bullets hit the upright. They cut a deep groove in its rotten length.

'Them shots came from two different directions, pard,' Ty said knowingly.

Shane pressed his back against the wall of the building and stared at the brutal scars the two bullets had made in the woodwork.

'Them shots came from a distance, Ty.' He spat. 'It ain't gunshots that did that. Them critters are shooting at us with carbines. No six-shooter's got that kinda range.'

Morrow edged to the corner of the building with his .45 gripped in his hand. He squinted hard but could not see anyone close by. He gave a nod of his head.

'You're right, Clint. Whoever is shooting at us has got range on their side. They have to be riflemen.' Morrow gritted his teeth and looked at the clouds of dust left in the wake of their terrified horses.

Shane moved next to Morrow.

'What we gonna do without our horses?' he asked. 'This land is deadly without horses.'

Morrow nodded.

31

'The horses will be back, Clint,' he reasoned. 'They'll get thirsty and come back for the water in the trough. There ain't nothing out there except sand and cactus. The nags will come back when they get the courage.'

Shane bit his lip. 'Yeah, you're right.'

'Our biggest problem is someplace out there, buddy.' Morrow pointed his gun.. 'We got us at least two riflemen shooting at us for some reason I ain't figured yet.'

'Could they be the four riders we saw earlier, Ty?' Shane wondered.

'Maybe,' Morrow said. 'I just can't work out why they didn't shoot us back in the desert if it was them, though. We had no cover out there. Why would they wait until we reached this ghost town to open up on us? It just don't figure.'

Clint Shane looked worried.

'Do you reckon there might be other critters around here, Ty?' he asked, gulping. 'Critters that intend killing us for some reason we don't know about yet?'

Morrow turned and looked at his friend.

'Yep,' he drawled.

Shane checked his gun and squinted at every

32

dune visible from the porch in which they were
sheltering.

'But what damn reason would anyone have for
shooting at us, Ty?' Shane wondered. 'We ain't
done them no harm, so why'd they start firing at
us?'

Morrow was thoughtful.

'They ain't just trying to scare us, Clint.
They're intending on burying us.'

'Hell!' Shane exhaled. 'You figure?'

Morrow nodded and moved along the boardwalk towards a half-rotten door which was barely
hanging on its hinges.

'They'd know that shooting at us would spook
our horses and leave us on foot. If they intended
scaring us off they'd have waited for us to be
mounted. Nope, they mean to kill us, Clint,'
Morrow told his partner.

Shane's face became drained of all colour as
he rested his spine against the wall.

'Why'd anyone want us dead?' he asked.

'When I've figured that out I'll tell you.'
Morrow nodded and kicked at the door. It fell
into a hundred bits of kindling. 'C'mon, Clint.
Let's see where this leads.'

They moved through the ramshackle interior

of what they both believed had been a hotel. As they came across a wide flight of steps the sound of rifle shots in the street echoed inside the building.

Morrow paused first and gazed at the staircase. His keen eyes darted up to the landing. He looked at Shane.

'We might get us a better view of them rifle-men if we head on up there, Clint,' he suggested.

Shane moved to his pal's shoulder and also looked up to the first of a row of a half-dozen doors. Neither of the men had ever seen cobwebs hanging like drapes before. He gave a nod.

'This place has sure seen better days, Ty,' Shane commented as his partner tested the first step with his dust-covered boot.

Morrow looked back at Shane.

'The steps seem strong enough to hold our weight without turning to sawdust,' he remarked as he slowly ascended the staircase. 'I'm gonna take me a look.'

'You ain't leaving me down here on my lone-some,' Shane said. Cautiously he followed his partner up the staircase towards the landing. The entire structure groaned and cracked beneath the steps of both men. Reaching the top, Morrow brushed the cobwebs aside and grunted. He gripped his six-shooter and studied the floorboards between himself and the first of the doors.

'Be careful of these boards, Clint,' Morrow warned. 'Some of them look damn weak.'

Shane gave a silent nod.

Morrow had been right to be cautious. Each step seemed to punch a hole into the weak wood beneath his boots.

He reached the door, turned its handle and pushed it into the empty room. Dust fell from the cracked ceiling as the door slammed against the wall. A strange smell greeted the two men. It was the smell of decay. Shafts of sunlight streamed from the windows into the room and appeared to dance as the dust drifted through them. Morrow glanced at the windows. Each had broken glass panes hanging from what remained of the frame.

Morrow strode towards the nearest window. Shane trailed him across the room until he reached its shattered remnants.

They stood at each side of the window and stared out across the ghost town. With the full sun reflecting off every surface the glare was blinding. Both men raised their hands to shield their eyes and looked at the high, rolling dunes that threatened to encroach on the dead town.

'Do you see them?' Morrow asked. 'I can't see nothing but damn sand.'

Shane shook his head slowly as he held his .45 at his side. Like his partner, he could see no sign of the men who had only just now been shooting at them.

'I can't see any of the riflemen, Ty,' he replied through gritted teeth.

'Where'd they go?' Morrow wondered.

Suddenly his question was answered. A bullet shattered one of the few remaining glass panes into a million fragments. The ear-splitting sound of rifle fire filled the room. In a mere second a hole was punched in the wall behind them. They were totally startled.

Morrow was first to regain his composure. He pointed out towards the undulating dunes. A cloud of gunsmoke drifted up into the cloudless sky.

'There's one of the varmints, Clint,' Morrow snarled, aiming his gun at the distant target. He squeezed its trigger over and over again until

Shane stopped him.

'You're wasting your time.' Shane shook his head. 'Our bullets ain't got the range, Ty.'

Another bullet carved its way through the window. Both men turned their backs as they became covered in debris.

Morrow snorted angrily.

'Damn it all!' he cursed angrily. 'We need our rifles to have any chance of picking them varmints off.'

Shane dusted himself off and stared at Morrow.

'Our rifles are still on our horses,' he said. 'Wherever they are.'

Morrow sighed.

Then the sound of yet another rifle shot shook the room as a lump of lead penetrated the wall above the window frame.

Morrow stared out of the window at the shooters. A thought came to him as his eyes vainly tried to see the riflemen clearly.

'They're firing at us as though they could see us, Clint,' he said. 'But how can they see anything from that far away?'

A bullet tore between the pair. Each man looked at the other in stunned awe.

'But they *can* see us,' Shane said.

Shielding his body against the side of the window, Morrow stared hard into the distance. He knew that Shane was right. The riflemen could see them.

'You're right,' Morrow said. 'I don't know how but they got us in their sights, Clint.'

'That just ain't possible.'

For a moment Morrow said nothing as he watched the smoke rise from where the riflemen were firing their weapons. Then he saw something.

Sun was glinting off glass.

Morrow turned to his friend.

'No wonder they can see us. One of them bastards has a telescopic sight on his damn Winchester,' he announced.

They turned away from the window, headed back to the passage and carefully negotiated a way to the top of the staircase.

'He's got himself a *what?*' Shane asked as both men hurried carefully down the stairs.

Morrow paused at the foot of the staircase and looked at his confused pal.

'A telescopic sight,' he repeated.

'What in tarnation is that?' Shane looked puzzled.

Morrow rolled his eyes. 'It's like a magnifying glass. You have heard of *them*, ain't you?'

Shane nodded firmly. 'I sure have.'

Morrow turned his head and studied the interior of the old building. Then he saw a busted door leading to the rear of the hotel. He pointed his gun.

'We're going that way. C'mon,' he said.

Like a faithful hound Shane trailed Morrow out of the gloomy interior of the building, out into the bright sunlit alley.

Morrow halted.

'They can't see us here,' he said. He turned full circle, looking for a safe place for both of them.

Shane rubbed the sweat from his face. 'Let's head on down to the back of the saloon. The townsfolk might have left a few bottles of whiskey in their hurry to get out of this town.'

Morrow nodded. 'That's good thinking, Clint. I could sure use a drink about now.'

They ran behind several of the empty buildings. This time it was Shane who took the lead. They used the shadows cast by the buildings as cover. Shane stopped first and drew his partner's attention to a large back wall.

'This is the saloon, Ty,' he said confidently.

Morrow looked at it. 'Are you sure?'

'I sure am.' Shane nodded. 'I noticed the front of this place when we was out in the street before the shooting started. The paint might have flaked off its old sign but there was enough remaining for me to figure what this place was.'

They moved in through a large hole in the rear wall and did not stop their progress until they reached the dusty interior of what was obviously a saloon. Just like the hotel, the interior was bedecked with dusty hanging cobwebs.

The bar room looked like a score of others that the two weary travellers had entered in other towns. The tables and chairs were still where the owner of the saloon had left them. The long bar counter stretched from one side of the room to the other. Morrow lifted the counter flap and walked into the place normally reserved for bartenders.

Dust and cobwebs covered virtually everything here, too. Shane trailed his pal and looked grimly at the flyblown clutter.

'They sure got themselves some real busy spiders around here, Ty,' he stammered. 'The one thing I hate most of all is spiders.'

40

'Hush up. They ain't as bad as critters with loaded carbines.' Morrow brushed cobwebs away from the shelves behind the counter with his free hand, then stopped as he found some bottles. Without hesitating for a single moment he lifted one of the bottles and blew at its dust-covered surface until he saw the whiskey label.

'The owner of this place must have been in one hell of a hurry to high-tail it out of this town, Clint,' he remarked, handing the bottle to Shane and lifting another. 'He must have fled with only what his arms could carry.'

'Lucky for us.' Shane smiled and raised the bottle to his mouth. He pulled the cork from the neck of the bottle with his teeth, then spat it away. The smell of whiskey filled the eager nostrils of both men.

Morrow lowered his own salvaged bottle from his lips and placed it down. He vaulted over the counter and made his way through the dusty furniture until he reached the locked door.

Shane finished his draught and watched as Morrow leaned against the door and lifted the blind away with his gun barrel. He said nothing as he made his way between the tables and chairs to where his pal was observing the street.

41

'The shooting's stopped, Clint,' Morrow observed, and stepped away from the door.

Shane took another swig from his bottle.

'I'd not celebrate too darn soon,' he warned.

Morrow holstered his gun. He was thoughtful as he paced around his friend. Shane had never seen Morrow look so concerned before.

'Without our horses we're stuck in this town,' Morrow muttered.

Shane rested his hip on a table and placed the bottle down beside him. He twirled his six-shooter and slid it neatly back into its leather holster.

'And them back-shooters got rifles,' he added.

'We've got rifles.' Morrow paused and looked at his pal. 'The trouble is, they're tucked under our saddles.'

Shane was thoughtful. 'I wonder where our horses are? They sure was running fast when they lit out.'

'They'll come back when they get thirsty.' Morrow repeated his earlier words.

'I sure hope they wait until after sundown, Ty,' Shane said. 'They'll get themselves shot for sure if they come trotting back in daylight.'

Morrow nodded. 'I reckon you're right.'

Shane did not seem to comprehend the gravity of the situation they were in. He gave out a belly laugh.

'You know something?' Shane said.

'What, Clint?'

'I got me a feeling we're in a fix.' He grinned.

Morrow smiled. 'You'll stop grinning when you get hungry.'

'There's gotta be grub in this town someplace, Ty,' Shane said. He pulled out his tobacco pouch and started making himself a smoke. 'All we gotta do is find it.'

Morrow looked at him and winced.

'Any grub we find here will be in the same condition as these buildings. Rotten.'

Shane rolled his smoke into shape and ran his tongue along the gummed edge of the paper.

'Canned grub don't rot,' he pointed out. He scratched a match along his pants leg and cupped its flame. He blew a line of smoke at the floor. 'You never thought about that, did you?'

Morrow accepted the tobacco pouch and started to roll a cigarette for himself.

'You're right, Clint. I never thought about canned grub.' He smiled.

Shane grinned like a cat that had found the cream.

'I'm not just a pretty face, you know?'

Morrow ran his tongue along the gummed strip of his cigarette paper and smoothed its length with his fingers. He placed it in the corner of his mouth.

'That's right, Clint. You ain't just a pretty face.'

Shane watched as Morrow slid a dust-covered chair from the table and sat down upon it. He pulled a match from his pants pocket and scratched it across the top of the table. He raised its flame to his cigarette and inhaled. The smoke filled his lungs as he sat staring at the floor.

'What's wrong, Ty?' Shane asked. 'We've been in worse scrapes than this before. Ain't no need to get sorrowful.'

Morrow pushed the brim of his Stetson off his temple and looked at his naive pal.

'How can a man get sorrowful when he's sitting in a saloon and don't have to pay for the whiskey, Clint?' He smiled and began to reload his gun.

Yet for all his bravado Morrow was worried. He sucked in more smoke and looked at the floor

44

once again. His mind was racing as it vainly tried to find a solution to their plight.

All he could think about was the riflemen.

THREE

There was an impressive nobility in the riders as they steered their bareback mounts winding through the dunes, which over the previous decades had progressed to the very edge of the ghost town. The riders had little apart from their aged weaponry and handsome buckskin clothing, but they still had the memories of what they had once been in this treacherous land. They travelled silently, like the phantoms to which their tribe had often been likened.

The dunes rose like petrified waves, towering over everything. The four braves guided their painted ponies along the narrow valleys between them using the shimmering heat haze as a shield. They had not intended to travel into the heart of trouble, but were forced to do so in order to collect the game and pelts they had secreted there.

The four mysterious horsemen had nothing to do with the shots that had trapped both Shane and Morrow in the ghost town. They were on a different mission. They could not afford the luxury of leaving their precious haul for there were many of their tribe who relied upon them not to return empty-handed.

Even though they knew the danger they were heading into the Cheyenne hunting party continued to snake through the dunes towards the ghost town. Earlier that day they had seemingly vanished from view as the two young drifters had made their dash for what they assumed was a living town, not one that was as dead as a graveyard.

The rifle fire that had frightened off Morrow's and Shane's mounts and had come close to killing them had not been from their carbines.

The four horsemen were more than capable of killing, but they did not unleash their venomous lead simply for the pleasure of destroying. They had an unwritten code, which they lived by. Only cowards killed merely because they could. It took brave men to face their enemies with no advantage, and the four riders were brave.

There were many well-armed riders in the West. Most thought that the more guns you carried the braver you were, but the opposite was usually closer to the truth. A coward with a gun can kill at distance without fear of retribution. The four riders carried only their hunting guns, and they were not cowardly.

Their code meant that they only killed game when they were hungry or on a quest to find food for their families. They never simply killed men for the joy of it, and never fired the first shot.

They regretted that their code was not shared by their enemies.

The southern Cheyenne had been driven from their homelands less than a generation before and were now forced to live in a land that was barren by comparison. The four horsemen were the best hunters of their tribe's dwindling numbers and had taken it upon themselves to travel far and wide in order to hunt the game they knew would nourish what was left of their once numerous people. As soon as they had been forced on to the reservation their people had been virtual prisoners.

It was never easy to watch a people who were said to be like phantoms. Their army captors had vainly attempted to do so but it was impossible.

The four-man hunting party regularly slipped out of the government-controlled reservation and moved into the forested hills and desert to find food and furs for their people. They had good reason to keep away from the prying eyes of any white men they encountered on their travels.

The last thing the Cheyenne needed was to be placed under even stricter control by their new would-be masters.

Earlier that afternoon the hunting party had by chance been spotted by Shane and Morrow as they too travelled through the dunes from the forest. The Cheyennes had used their knowledge of the vast uncharted terrain to disappear from the sight of Morrow and Shane with an ease which seemed uncanny.

The Indians did not wish to be discovered before they had had a chance to collect the game they had hidden and make their way back to the reservation.

Just like mountain pumas, they killed their game and buried it until they were ready to return to the arid reservation.

The unexpected sight of the young riders had forced the Cheyenne hunters to change their plans and take a long detour through the perilous desert.

When the shooting started all they knew for sure was that the riflemen were ahead of them, directly between themselves and the game they had to collect.

As they rode their ponies among the dunes they were curious as to who was shooting and why.

On each of their stealthy excursions they had tried to avoid all contact with white men, to remain unseen and undisturbed. However, they had glimpsed both Shane and Morrow, and did not believe that these young horsemen would be the shooters.

If anything, they thought, Morrow and Shane were the targets.

This notion rested uneasily in the hearts of the four Cheyennes. Their eyes had witnessed too many massacres in times past, and they were something they would never forget.

They knew how to use their weapons but doubted if either of the youngsters shared their ability. Every shot that rang out across the desert

was like listening to another slaughter of innocents.

The Cheyenne hunting party used every
natural scrap of cover the scorching desert could
offer them to move ever closer to the place from
where the deafening shots rang out.

In spite of all the multitude of wrongs the
white men had done to their noble people the
four warriors could not quell their natural
instincts and ignore what they had seen. Brave
men faced their demons; they never turned tail
and ran away. It was obvious that evil men were
trying to kill the two youngsters whom they had
seen earlier, and that awareness was burning into
their souls.

They guided their unshod mounts towards the
noise of the brutal rifle shots. Few men could
ever have equalled the skill these warriors had
with their rifles or bows, should they care to use
them.

Like phantoms they continued silently to steer
their four horses towards the whiff of gunsmoke.

FOUR

The sun beat down without mercy on everything and everyone beneath its unremitting rays. A noisome vapour rose all around the three riflemen who moved across the dunes, closer to the town that lay just beyond. They stopped on the hot white surface of the dunes and stared down in search of the pair of young men whom they had yet to dispatch. They huddled in a sweaty bunch, a quarter of a mile from the edge of the ghost town and surveyed every inch of the sun-scorched settlement. Once again they had lost sight of their prey. They cursed the fact that they had not managed to kill them yet.

Somehow they had missed a dozen chances to kill both Shane and Morrow, and they were becoming more and more angry.

They blamed the sun as it slowly traversed the cloudless blue sky for their misfortune and inaccuracy. They cursed the shimmering heat haze, which mocked their eyes as they stared down through their rifle sights. There were countless reasons why they had so far failed to hit their targets.

Whatever the truth of their failure was, none of them could have ever accepted it. They killed without guilt or mercy, and whenever they missed those at whom they aimed their lethal armoury they blamed it on bad luck.

The trio of hardened bandits crouched just below the top of a smooth sand dune and methodically started to reload their rifles' magazines with bullets from the ammunition belts that criss-crossed their chests.

These men were so well armed that they could have taken on a troop of cavalry without running out of bullets. To take on two youngsters seemed no harder than swatting flies by comparison.

As they sat beneath the shade of their wide-brimmed sombreros the acrid stench of soiled skin rose unnoticed by the three bandits.

Pancho Cruz was the unofficial leader of the

small group and, by all accounts of his atrocities, the most deadly. It was said that in the previous ten years he had killed more than fifty men, women and children. The truth was even worse, for he was not shy of using dynamite when his bullets failed to kill his enemies swiftly enough.

Cruz finished loading his Winchester and stared from beneath his black bushy eyebrows at his two followers.

The youngest of the three was known as Juan Sanchez. He killed when told to kill. He had ridden with Cruz since the last revolution and was one of that rare breed of men who did exactly what he was told to do. There was little brain beneath his sombrero but there was loyalty.

The third bandit was called Francisco Lopez. He was roughly the same age as Cruz but that was where the similarity ended. Unlike their leader, Lopez had no ambition to do anything except drink, ravage females and kill men. He had been known to do all three and then eat his fill of his victim's chilli. Lopez always carried a long stiletto in his left boot to add misery to his slaughtering.

All three rested their newly reloaded weapons against their legs and pondered on the two strangers they had been shooting at. What had started as a simple task had grown into a headache for the bandits.

They knew that they should have ended the lives of the young riders long before now. Shane and Morrow had somehow evaded every single bullet they had blasted at them and that was starting to rile the deadly trio.

Lopez looked down the dune at their three horses tied securely to a cactus trunk. He then turned to Cruz.

'Who are the men that we are trying to kill, Pancho?' he asked. With his teeth he ripped a chunk of tobacco from a block he kept at all times hidden in his shirt front.

'They are nothing, Francisco,' Cruz replied to the chewing Lopez. 'They are merely an obstruction.'

Sanchez pushed his battered sombrero off his forehead and looked at Cruz.

'They are a *what*, Pancho?'

Cruz checked his pistols and simplified his words. 'They are in our way, Juan.'

'So we are going to kill them for being in our way?' Lopez wondered as his mind tried to understand.

'*Sí*, Francisco.' Cruz nodded. 'They are in the

town and we want to enter the town without getting shot at. The easiest way to do this is to kill them.'

Both his followers nodded.

'Why do we want to enter the ghost town, Pancho?' Sanchez asked. 'I forget.'

Cruz rolled on to his knees and stroked the telescopic sight set on his rifle. It was as though the devilish bandit were caressing a female's soft body.

'Do you not remember the treasure we left buried down there after we chased all the people away, *amigos*?' he asked his forgetful followers.

Again both his men nodded.

'Now it is time for us to collect that treasure.' Cruz spoke angrily as he pondered on the delay. 'Those two gringos might find it before we can dig it up. We cannot allow this. So they have to die.'

'They cannot last long down there.' Lopez laughed. 'Their horses ran away when we started shooting. Nobody can live out here for very long without horses, Pancho.'

Cruz looked angry. 'They should be dead already. We should have killed them before they reached the ghost town.'

'But we did not arrive here until after they had ridden into it, Pancho,' Lopez pointed out.

'I know, Francisco,' Cruz snarled, sounding like a rabid dog. 'If only we had arrived sooner. We would have greeted them with bullets before they had time to hide.'

Sanchez nodded in agreement. '*Sí, amigo.* You are right.'

'Those stinking gringos stand between us and our treasure, *amigos*.' Cruz snorted angrily. 'I do not permit this. It is *our* money, stolen from many rich people. We must kill those two gringos quickly.'

Sanchez smiled, showing his blackened teeth.

'So they have to die?'

Cruz tightened the drawstring under his chin and stood up.

'*Sí, amigo.* They have to die,' he confirmed.

'Good.' Sanchez laughed as he rose to his feet. 'I like nothing better than killing gringos.'

'Before we are through,' Cruz expanded, 'you shall be able to kill many more stinking gringos.'

Sanchez laughed excitedly.

'I am getting very hungry, Pancho,' Lopez complained as he too stood on the sandy slope beside his leader. 'When do we eat?'

Pancho Cruz rested his rifle on his shoulder. His black eyes glanced down on the ghost town.

'Soon, Franciso. Very soon,' he replied. Then he snapped his fingers at Sanchez. 'Bring our horses. I am tired of crawling on my belly like a sidewinder. It is time for us to attack and kill those gringos.'

Sanchez made his way down the shifting sand towards their tethered horses with a gleeful excitement that belied what he and his cohorts intending doing.

Cruz yanked the lever of his rifle and primed it once again. His cold eyes glinted like rough diamonds from beneath his sombrero.

Lopez spat out a lump of black goo and wiped the spittle from his mouth with the back of his sleeve. He pulled the long slim knife from his boot and stared at its honed edge as his thumb caressed its blade.

'Can I cut their hearts out of their chests, Pancho?' he asked the bandit leader. 'I have never seen a gringo's heart before.'

Cruz nodded.

'*Sí*, Francisco. You know I never stop you enjoying yourself, *amigo*.' He smiled.

The bandit leader walked up to the top of the

white dune and glared down at the weather-beaten buildings. Somewhere in one of them Morrow and Shane were about to get company. He raised his rifle above his head and squeezed its trigger viciously. The deafening shot echoed all around the desolate terrain. Cruz laughed out loud and shook his Winchester as though it were a club.

He fired again at the cloudless sky.

The noise of the shot reverberated for what seemed an eternity. It was a warning to the two men who were trapped inside the small ghost town.

A warning of impending doom.

FIVE

Five miles from the ghost town a cloud of hoof dust rose up through the trees into the sky as a small contingent of troopers steered their horses down towards the desert. Each of the enlisted men trailed Captain Ezra Blake through the trees towards the edge of the desert in single file. The difference in temperature was drastic as the sun-scorched sand sent heat upward into the shimmering air. Blake raised his gauntlet and shouted his orders back to the six cavalrymen.

'Halt!' he commanded. He stopped his mount and listened to the ominous sound of rifle shots as they rang out around them.

The seven horsemen drew rein while still a few yards inside the forest. They held their mounts in check just behind the tail of Blake's horse. Sergeant Dom Riley tapped his spurs and steered his own mount beside that of the stern-faced captain.

'More shots, Captain,' Riley growled, sounding like a bear.

'I heard them, Riley,' Blake snapped. He was working out where the shots had come from. He glanced through the last of the trees at the shimmering dunes and pointed. 'They came from down there.'

'That they did,' Riley agreed.

Blake narrowed his eyes. 'Any idea what's down there?'

'No, sir.' Riley shrugged his powerful shoulders. 'I've never been to this godforsaken place before.'

The captain twisted on his saddle and looked at the troopers behind them.

'Do any of you men know what's down there?'

There was a general shaking of the soldiers' heads.

Blake turned his gaze towards the heat haze. 'The shooting has stopped, Riley,' he observed.

Sergeant Riley nodded.

'That it has, Captain,' he agreed. 'Probably

just a couple of hunters. Nothing for us to get concerned about.'

'I wouldn't give those shots a second thought if I hadn't heard a dozen more of them during the last hour, Riley,' Blake said. He quenched his thirst from his canteen. 'Hunters don't keep shooting carbines at their prey. Not for over an hour, anyway.'

'Unless the prey has only two legs?' Riley raised his eyebrows.

'Exactly,' Blake replied. He raised his canteen to his lips again and this time took a long slow drink. Then he secured its stopper. 'Men tend to take a lot more killing than dumb animals.'

'That they do, Captain,' Riley agreed.

Captain Blake hung his canteen back on his saddle horn and rested his gauntleted knuckles on his hips. He was deep in thought. At last he turned to Riley.

'It has to be the four Cheyenne bucks we're hunting, Sergeant,' he said. 'We've tracked them to this point. I reckon they've started attacking some unfortunate white folks.'

Riley leaned across the distance between them. He looked hard into his superior's face and shook his head in disagreement.

'With due respect, Captain,' he started, 'those rifle shots didn't come from the kinda guns those bucks have got.'

Blake had never liked anyone who contradicted him. His eyes narrowed and burned into the face of his sergeant.

'I'm telling you it has to be the Cheyennes, Riley,' he insisted.

Riley had risen to the rank of sergeant by always agreeing with his superiors, but this time he knew that Blake was totally wrong. He shook his head even more violently.

'It can't have been, Captain,' he growled.

'Why not?'

'I'll tell you why not. The Cheyenne bucks we're looking for have only reservation-supplied Henrys, Captain,' Riley told the officer. 'The shots we heard came from much finer rifles, which them Injuns ain't got.'

Blake stared at the burly sergeant sitting alongside him.

'Rifles are rifles, Riley.'

Riley shook his head. 'I don't know much, Captain, but I do know about rifles. The shots we just heard came from Winchesters. Brand-new Winchesters is my bet.'

Blake inhaled deeply.

'Winchesters?'

'Yep, Winchesters.' Riley nodded. 'White Horse and the other Cheyennes have only old Henrys to shoot with. They sound completely different. They got a much tinnier sound altogether.'

Blake cleared his throat. Reluctantly he said,

'So it wasn't the Cheyennes that were doing the firing?'

Riley beamed. 'It sure weren't. Whoever is shooting them Winchesters is someone else.'

Then, to the utter surprise of Riley and the rest of the cavalry riders, Blake said,

'It doesn't matter one bit, Riley. Whoever was doing the shooting, it doesn't alter the fact that we're on the trail of these Cheyenne bucks. They've left the reservation and have to be stopped before they do any damage.'

Riley was a lot more seasoned than his officer.

'If you ask me, I reckon them bucks are only out hunting for fresh game for the old and young 'uns of their tribe, Captain,' he opined. 'The Indian agent is rumoured to be starving those Injuns, sir. White Horse and his bucks are just collecting grub.'

64

Blake looked at Riley in horror. 'Are you sympathizing with the Cheyennes?'

Riley shook his head.

'Nope, but I don't think it's right for us to be tracking them down for just doing what any of us would do,' he averred.

Captain Blake raised his fist and shook it under the nose of the brawny sergeant.

'Never disagree with me, Riley,' he warned furiously. 'If you do I'll see that you lose those stripes. Do you understand me?'

Riley averted his eyes. 'Yes, sir.'

Filled with satisfaction Blake looked over the head of his horse at the terrain in front of them.

'Those stinking Cheyennes left the reservation without permission, Riley,' Blake said with a sigh. 'The Indian agent told us to track them down and, if necessary, kill them. I consider this is probably the best solution.'

Sergeant Riley rubbed his whiskers.

'Are you sure about that, sir?'

'Of course I'm sure, Riley. You have to consider the facts. They are filthy Indians and can never be trusted. The Indian wars taught us that, didn't they?'

Riley sighed heavily. 'I fought in them wars, sir.

We never had no trouble with the southern Cheyennes.'

Blake had never set foot in this land until he was posted to Fort Dodge, only six months previously. Like so many of his kind he was filled with colourful notions but was very short of practical experience.

'I don't believe that for one moment,' Blake disagreed.

'Why not, Captain?' Riley asked.

'They're still Indians, Sergeant.' Blake shouted as though he had a bad taste in his mouth. 'Stinking redskins that don't have any idea of civilized behaviour. Given half a chance they'll scalp, rape and heaven knows what other atrocities they'll conceive in their twisted minds. No white people are safe with them on the loose. They're savages, Riley. We have to stop them in case they do commit any of these crimes. It's our duty.'

Dom Riley glanced over his muscular shoulder and whistled at the troopers. He had given up all hope of reasoning with the immature officer.

'Get ready.' He smiled at the faces of the soldiers. The troopers lowered their canteens and tightened the stoppers before readying themselves.

66

'Are the men ready, Sergeant?' Blake asked.

'They're ready, Captain.' Riley nodded.

Just as he had been taught in military school, Captain Blake waved his gauntlet, a satisfied smirk etched in his dust-caked features.

'Forward ho!' he bellowed, and spurred his horse to walk forward.

Riley winked at the troopers.

'You heard the good captain, boys,' he said, then added in expert mockery: 'Forward ho!'

The short line of cavalrymen emerged from the trees and followed their captain down into the desert. Soon the dunes were towering over them just as they had done to Shane and Morrow earlier.

The troopers rode deeper into the inferno of sand.

SIX

The two young drifters made their move. They emerged from the side door of the saloon and cautiously ventured up the alleyway, back towards the main street. With each long stride they envisaged their unseen adversaries' rifles cutting them down. The more experienced Morrow led the way until they reached the main street once again. Morrow glanced up and down its length. There was no sign of the riflemen, nor of their own precious horses.

Nothing but tumbleweed rolled across the white sand.

Shane sighed as he vainly tried to see a hint of the rifles up among the dunes.

'You figure they're still up there someplace, Ty?' he asked.

Morrow nodded his head. 'I sure do. Critters like that ain't easy to shake off, Clint. Keep your eyes wide open and shoot if'n you see them.'

Shane rubbed the sweat from his face. 'I reckon I won't be blinking for the longest while, Ty.'

They slid like sidewinders round the corner, stepped up on to the boardwalk and started to move through the shadows below the porch overhang.

'Keep your eyes peeled, Clint,' Morrow instructed, as he gripped on to his trusty .45. 'Them varmints might be anywhere by now. They might even be down here in the town.'

Shane looked fearfully all around them. 'They could be down here?'

'Sure they could,' Morrow replied, and ventured forward. 'They ain't had much joy at killing us from up there on them dunes, have they? Sooner or later they've gotta come down here and try to get us in their sights.'

They both moved from the front of one building to the next. The shadows cast down by the overhangs gave them some relief from the intense heat. They paused and pressed their backs against the fragile front of one of the abandoned stores.

'Do you figure we'll find us some grub soon, Ty?' Shane asked. He too was keeping close to the rotted structure. 'This heat is making me plumb tired. There has to be some canned goods in this town, don't there?'

'I sure hope so,' Morrow replied. 'You ain't the only one that's hungry.'

They continued on until they were close to the end of the boardwalk. Morrow paused and stared in the direction from where they had both witnessed the shooting originate. They had no sooner cast their attention at the dune that towered over even the highest of the buildings than half a dozen bolts of lightning came at them through the heat haze.

'Holy smoke!' Morrow yelled out as the wooden uprights next to them were peppered with lead and exploded into a million splinters.

Barely able to believe that the rifle bullets had missed them Morrow shook the fragments off himself and stared up at the three men standing upon the ridge of the mountain of sand.

'There they are, Clint.' Morrow pointed with

his gun. Then he pulled his trigger finger back. A red flash erupted from the gun, followed by a circle of smoke. Morrow prided himself of his skill with his gun but, to his horror, he saw the sand kick up as his bullet fell well short.

Shane rose to his feet and coughed, trying to rid his lungs of the choking dust he had inhaled.

'We still ain't got their range, Ty,' he spluttered.

Morrow's eyes widened as he watched the men ready their carbines once more. He grabbed Shane and started to run across the wide street. They heard the sound of the rifles being fired as soon as they reached halfway across the wide deserted thoroughfare. The ground around both men erupted as bullets tore into the sand.

Then, just as they were within ten feet of the boardwalk, Shane gave out a sickening, agonized groan as he was knocked off his feet.

Morrow stopped and looked back at his pal. The dust-caked shirt Shane was wearing suddenly turned vivid crimson.

'Clint!' he gasped at his motionless friend.

There was no answer.

SEVEN

The rifle fire stopped for a moment yet its menacing echoes resounded off every decaying wall in the ghost town. Then another more horrifying noise replaced the deafening shots. It was the yells of the jubilant bandits resounding over the ghost town as Pancho Cruz and his deadly cohorts celebrated the fact that they had finally managed to pick off one of the two drifters who stood between them and their treasure.

Morrow had reached the safety of the opposite side of the wide street but his partner had not. Morrow gasped in horror at the sight of his blood-soaked pal. The blazing sun burned down upon his unmoving friend. Morrow knew that to run back out into the street was risky but his own safety was not the priority here: his pal's life was.

It might be suicidal, but Shane was doomed if Morrow left him where he lay. He tossed his hat aside and prepared himself for the short but possibly fatal dash. Morrow listened to the joyous bandits. So far they had not started to fire their lethal Winchesters at the defenceless body.

He knew he had to act and act now.

Morrow rammed his gun back into its holster. He summoned every scrap of his courage, then bolted out from the shadows into the sunlight. Moving from side to side in an attempt to avoid being back-shot, he ran for all he was worth towards the seemingly lifeless body stretched out on the bloody sand.

He had only just reached Shane when he heard the bandits stop their triumphant laughter. They had seen him, he thought. As Morrow reached down and swept Shane up in his arms he heard the sound of the rifles being cranked into operation again. He ducked and hoisted Shane up on to his shoulder. Morrow had turned on his boot heels and started to run when the shooting resumed. A bullet tore the fabric of his sleeve, yet he kept on running to where he had left his hat.

Soon more bullets kicked sand up all around

him as his long legs staggered under the weight of his friend. The ground burst like an erupting volcano around Morrow's boots. He kept on running until he reached the sanctuary of the shaded side of the wide street. Only then did he fall on to his knees and allow Shane to fall from his shoulder on to the boardwalk.

Morrow was covered in blood.

It was not his.

Frantically he moved on his knees beside his pal and stared at Shane. There was no sign of life apart from a shallow movement of Shane's chest. The young drifter had a brutal graze across the side of his head. Only the Stetson had prevented it from entering Shane's skull. Blood flowed freely from the wound and stained his face.

Morrow tore his own bandanna from his neck and tied it around Shane's head. Then he hastily turned the unconscious figure on to his back and looked for other wounds.

He did not have to search too hard.

The blood-soaked sleeve guided Morrow's eyes to the hole high in Shane's shoulder. The shirt had been brutally torn from his flesh as the rifle bullet found its target.

As he tended his friend Morrow was well aware

74

that the riflemen had stopped shooting. He plugged the hole in Shane's shoulder, then looked all around for somewhere to go. As his mind raced he picked up his hat and returned it to his head.

'And you wanted to be a deputy,' Morrow sighed at his pal.

He looked at his unconscious friend. He had slowed the flow of blood but Morrow knew that wherever he went Shane would leave a trail of blood in his wake. He pressed the makeshift wadding deeper into the bullet hole in Shane's shoulder, then rubbed his neck as he heard something break the silence out among the dunes.

It was a sound that could only be made by saddle gear. The riflemen were now on horseback, he told himself. The noise was being carried across the dunes as horses chewed on bits and spurs jabbed the animals' flesh.

'Damn it all! They're coming,' Morrow said.

Knowing that he had to take his partner somewhere safe if they were both going to avoid the Mexicans' wrath, Morrow rested one boot beside Shane and then slid his arms under his pal. He was about to lift him when Shane suddenly

75

awoke and lashed out with his fists.

'Are you OK, Clint?' Morrow gasped and straightened up.

Barely awake, Shane looked through bleary eyes until he recognized Morrow.

'It's you, Ty. I had me the strangest nightmare. Someone was shooting at us,' he mumbled.

Morrow helped his pal up off the boardwalk and steadied him. 'That weren't no nightmare, buddy. There are folks shooting at us and they plumb hit you.'

Shane blinked as though he were trying to rid his brain of the throbbing war drums which filled his cracked skull. He raised his hand and winced as his gloved fingers touched the graze.

'Where are they?' he asked.

'Close, Clint,' Morrow told him as he led Shane down through a gap between two of the crumbling buildings. 'Too damn close.'

EIGHT

There was no sign of any of the men who had opened up with their high-powered carbines, yet the sound of their saddle leather grew louder with every beat of the two youngsters' pounding hearts. Morrow had practically carried his friend from the boardwalk and down towards the rear of the deserted buildings. He rested Shane against a wall and moved round it to gain a better idea of where they might seek shelter. Shane stared out on to the bright sun-baked scene as his pal returned.

'Can you see them, Ty?' he asked weakly.

'Nope, but that don't mean they ain't close, Clint,' Morrow wisely answered. 'Trouble is, we don't know how many of them there are or which way they're coming. All I know for sure is that I seen three of the varmints.'

'Three?' Shane rested against the wall as his friend vainly tried to figure out where the horsemen were. 'That don't sound a lot.'

Morrow glanced at his friend. Blood still dripped from the hideous wounds even though Shane seemed unaware of how badly injured he actually was. Morrow pressed a hand against the chest of his wounded pal and steadied him.

'Three ain't a lot, Clint,' he replied in a confident tone.

'We can take them, Ty,' Shane said.

'Sure we can,' Morrow agreed. 'Anyone can shoot rifles with telescopic sights. Once they get down here we'll find out exactly how brave they really are.'

Shane mustered all his strength and staggered to the side of his pal. 'Who are these critters, Ty? Have you any idea who they are?'

'By my reckoning they're Mexican bandits,' Morrow replied. 'I seen their hats. Big and wide.'

'Sombreros?' Shane suggested.

'Yep, that's what they was wearing,' Morrow replied. Supporting his pal he moved round to the rear of one of the buildings, towards a large set of wooden steps that led up to a veranda which seemed to encircle the structure. 'This looks like some kinda hotel.'

Shane blinked hard. 'It sure does.'

Morrow paused when he reached the bottom of the flight of wooden steps. He wrapped his arm around Shane's waist and pointed.

'Are you up to climbing these steps, Clint?' Morrow knew that their best bet was to get up as high as they could if they were to stand a chance against the men who were determined to kill them. 'It's a long way up, but I figure we'll be a whole lot safer there.'

Shane looked at his partner's face. 'My legs are the only things that ain't giving me grief, Ty. Let's get up there. I feel kinda exposed out here.'

Both men ascended the wooden steps. Each step seemed to creak as they climbed slowly towards the veranda. When they reached the veranda Morrow held his partner's weight and searched for somewhere safe to take him.

Shane pointed at one of the doors. 'Let's go in there. At least we'll be out of sight once we get inside.'

Morrow did not argue.

He helped his friend to the door and carefully

took hold of its rusted handle. The door was in little better shape than most of the rest of the town. The two men walked along what appeared to be a hotel corridor. There were several doors to either side of them, each with flaking paint and bearing corroded room numbers. At the end of the corridor there was a window, which looked out on to the veranda and the main street.

Morrow turned the handle on the last door and entered the room, which had a window that also looked out on to the veranda and the street. Morrow kicked the door shut and moved towards a cot. He helped Shane sit down on the mattress and then moved towards the window. Every pane of glass had fallen from the frame as the desert heat had dried out its putty.

Morrow glanced briefly at Shane. 'Are you OK?'

'I'm fine,' Shane lied.

'We ought to be safe in here for a while,' Morrow said. He dragged a chair towards the window and sat down. 'I wonder where they'll come into this town. The dunes will slow them up a tad but they'll show soon.'

'Do you reckon we've got a chance, Ty?' Shane asked.

'Sure we have,' Morrow replied, but he too asked himself the same question.

Shane suddenly noticed the hole in his shoulder and tried to flex his fingers. The muscles in his right arm were twisted in reaction to the hideous bullet, which still rested against his bones. He stared along his blood-soaked sleeve at his hand. It no longer looked like a hand, but resembled a claw.

'I seem to have me a lump of lead in my shoulder, Ty,' he said fearfully. 'I can't move my hand. My fingers are all crippled up.'

Ty Morrow glanced at his pal. He knew that the youngster was scared and tried to make light of the problem.

'Quit fretting. Reckon if we're still alive when this is over I might try to cut that bullet out for you, Clint.' Morrow pulled the spent casings from his still warm gun and replaced them with fresh shells from his belt. 'You were always a lousy shot anyway.'

Shane sighed heavily. 'You're gonna cut the bullet out, huh? That sounds real dandy, Ty. I can hardly wait.'

The pounding of approaching horses' hoofs filled the room as the bandits drew closer.

Morrow said nothing, but he leaned through the window and looked in both directions before returning to his seat. He snapped his gun together and glanced at his pal.

He had never seen Shane look so weak before.

'Them varmints are coming, ain't they?' Shane said.

Morrow cocked his gun hammer and nodded.

'They're coming,' he said.

Shane blinked painfully. 'I sure hope I find out why them bastards have been using us for target practice before they kill us, Ty.'

Morrow smiled.

'We ain't dead yet, buddy,' he drawled.

Clint Shane exhaled loudly.

'Why do you reckon total strangers want to kill us so badly, Ty? Folks don't just start shooting at other folks for no reason. It don't make no sense. No sense at all.'

Morrow was thoughtful as he chewed on his friend's words and considered them.

'You're right, Clint.' He smiled. 'Folks don't usually start shooting at other folks for no reason.'

Shane looked bewildered. 'I just said that.'

'Think about what you said, Clint. For them

critters to start shooting at us just after we rode into this ghost town don't make any sense unless you think on it,' Morrow explained.

Shane looked no less confused. 'I've been thinking about it and it still don't make no sense.'

Morrow leaned close to his pal.

'Ask yourself why they're shooting,' he suggested. 'They don't know us. We don't know them. There can only be one reason why they're so all-fired intent on killing us, Clint.'

'What's the reason, Ty?'

Morrow looked down from the hotel window, then returned his attention to his friend.

'There's something here in this ghost town. Something mighty important. So important that them rifle-toting varmints want to get their hands on it so bad they'll kill anyone who gets in their way,' he reasoned. 'Us being here has put a fox in their hen house. We could be anyone and them bastards would still be trying to kill us.'

Shane bit his lip.

'You reckon they've got something hid in this broken-down town?' he asked. 'Something valuable?'

Morrow rubbed the steel barrel of his six-shooter against his jaw and continued to listen to the drumming of the bandits' mounts as they grew louder.

'Yep. That's what I reckon,' he said. 'I could be wrong but men who try to kill strangers must have themselves a mighty big motive.'

Shane nodded slowly. 'It makes sense to me. I reckon you're dead right. There must be something real valuable hid in this town someplace.'

Morrow straightened up and pointed his gun out of the window.

'They must have hid something around here someplace, thinking that nobody would ever find it coz nobody would ever ride into a ghost town, Clint.'

'We did.' Shane held his good hand against his bloody temple.

Ty Morrow shrugged. 'We rode in here by accident.'

Shane swallowed hard.

'How do you figure we're gonna get out of this scrape, Ty?' he asked. 'You saw three Mexicans, but there might be a heap more.'

Morrow gritted his teeth.

'We'll get out of this, Clint,' he said. 'Don't you go fretting about that. I'll stop them.'

'We ain't gunfighters, Ty,' Shane mumbled.

'They'll kill you just like they've done for me. You gotta try and get out of here while you still can.'

Morrow looked across the room at his pal.

'How can I ride out of here?' he said. 'I ain't got a horse. Besides I couldn't leave you here on your lonesome.'

'Why not?' Shane stared through blurred eyes at his pal and forced a smile. 'I'd leave you here if the tables were turned.'

'You would?' Morrow raised an eyebrow.

'Well, I might.' Shane lowered his head and stared at the droplets of blood which continued to drip from the gash on the side of his head. He looked back at Morrow. 'What's your plan for killing them Mexicans?'

Morrow bit his lip. 'I figure on shooting them.'

'That ain't much of a plan, Ty.' Shane shrugged.

'It's the only one I've got,' Morrow admitted.

Suddenly Morrow heard the horses below his vantage point and swung back to the window. He stared down over the veranda at the sight of the three rifle-toting horsemen as they rode past the hotel. All he could see clearly from the window was their sombreros.

'They're here,' he whispered.

Shane stared at his clawed hand and cursed his infirmity as he failed to be able even to reach his holstered .45.

'Damn it all. They done crippled me, Ty. I ain't gonna be able to help you.'

Morrow rushed across the room and drew Shane's gun from the holster. He placed it in his friend's left hand and nodded.

'Don't you fire that damn gun until one of them critters is looming over you. Right?' he instructed.

Shane nodded wearily. 'What are you figuring on doing?'

'I ain't sure.' Morrow moved back to the window and cautiously looked out. He could see the bandits riding to the far end of the street. Their Winchesters were resting upon their thighs as the trio steered their mounts towards the trough of water.

'Where are they now?' Shane asked.

'By the trough I filled with that pump,' Morrow replied. He raised his gun, closed one eye and aimed it at the bandits.

'If you miss you'll bring the whole bunch down on us, Ty,' Shane warned.

Morrow lowered his gun. 'You're right, Clint. I

can't let the critters know where we are. They'd probably burn this hotel down with us in it.'

Shane leaned on the brass bedpost. 'You gotta shoot and move, Ty. Shoot at them and then run for cover. Don't give them a target. You also gotta get a lot closer.'

Even though Shane was barely conscious, Morrow knew that he was talking a lot of sense. The trouble was that to do what Shane suggested would force him to leave Shane alone in this hotel room.

'You're right, buddy,' Morrow said.

Shane smiled weakly. 'Go get 'em, Ty.'

That was all the encouragement Morrow needed to leave his friend. He stepped out of the window on to the veranda and crouched as low as possible. He focused on the three horsemen at the far end of the street; they were refilling their canteens whilst their horses drank.

Tumbleweed rolled down the long thoroughfare as if by magic as Morrow looked around the area. He had to follow Shane's advice.

The only way to survive a gunfight with seasoned gunmen was to shoot and run. Morrow knew he was not good enough with his .45 to risk a showdown.

He nodded to himself.

Shoot and run, he kept thinking.

Morrow ran along the veranda towards the end rail. When he reached the railing he stepped up on to it and jumped across to an adjacent building.

The wooden shingles absorbed the impact of his landing. He scrambled up the roof until he reached its ridge. Then, taking his life in his hands, Morrow slid down the shingles and threw himself across the gap between them and the next building. He landed on a flat roof and sprinted to a black metal chimney stack.

When he reached the stack he dropped on to one knee and raised his gun. He aimed at the three riflemen.

This time he had the range, his mind told him. Now he had the advantage.

They were unaware that one of their chosen targets now had the drop on them for a change. Yet as he aimed his six-shooter Morrow realized that it takes a certain type of person to kill in cold blood.

He swallowed, but there was no spittle in his dry throat.

Sweat rolled down his face from under the

brim of his hat as he kept a bead on the bandits.

'Shoot,' he whispered to himself as his hand began to shake. 'Shoot the back-shooters before they see you.'

Yet no matter how hard he tried, he was unable to pull on his trigger. Slowly he began to lower his gun as it dawned on him that he was no mindless killer.

As he shook his head in confused disgust with himself he was brought back to reality by the raised voices. His head jolted back up just in time to see the bandits raising their Winchesters.

The men were yelling at the tops of their voices but Morrow did not understand a word of their lingo. They were shouting to one another in Mexican.

Before he had time to move away from the edge of the flat rooftop he heard the deafening *rat-tat-tat* of rifle fire. Hot flashes of lethal lead exploded from the barrels and came hurtling through the dry air at him. Before Morrow had time to move the bullets hit the metal chimney stack, sending splinters in all directions like loco fireflies.

Morrow fell backwards as the stack crashed on top of him, covering him with years-old black soot. Coughing, Morrow turned and frantically scrambled away from the edge of the rooftop, realizing that if he did not do something fast their bullets would surely kill him.

From his high position Morrow could see the Mexicans clearly for the first time. His heart sank as his narrowed eyes focused on the trio of obviously deadly killers. Cruz and his cohorts looked more vicious even than Morrow had imagined anyone could look.

Their defiant stance told him that, unlike him, they were unafraid. The crossed belts of ammunition they sported on their chests looked like suits of armour as the sun danced across the countless bullets they harboured. Pancho Cruz was laughing as he and his men fired their repeating rifles at him.

They were having fun with him, as though he were a defenceless animal they were taking potshots at. For the first time in his life Morrow knew that he had bitten off more than he could chew.

He rolled on to his belly and squeezed his trigger. The .45 blasted a bullet down into the street. He had no idea where his shot had actually gone but, seeing that none of the three bandits moved an inch, he assumed he had not even come close to hitting any of them.

Morrow desperately fired again. The dense cloud of gunsmoke that spewed from his gun barrel blinded him from his targets. He rolled over until he found clean air, only to see the Winchesters all fire back at him at the same time. The parapet around the flat roof shattered into a thousand fragments of smouldering debris.

Morrow ducked.

The ash showered down on him. Morrow cocked his hammer and fired again. Then he backed away from the edge of the rooftop, and got to his feet again. He thought about his injured pal and knew that whilst the bandits were shooting at *him* Shane was safe.

His mind raced.

Shane had told him to shoot and run, he remembered.

He'd done some shooting and now it was time to run.

Morrow heard the rifles being cranked into readiness again and knew that at any moment their lethal bullets would come seeking him. He looked to his left at the steep shingle roof from which he had jumped earlier and knew it was impossible for him to return the way he had come. Morrow looked to his right and realized that the gap was far too great for him to reach the building there.

There was only one way he could go.

Morrow gripped his gun tightly in his hand and sprinted for all he was worth towards the back of the flat roof. Then he heard the bandits fire their rifles again. He could feel the heat of their lead as it passed over him.

Morrow raced across the flat surface towards the rear of the building. He had no idea what lay over the parapet on that side of the building, but he reckoned that it had to be a lot safer than remaining here in the line of fire.

He reached the parapet and leapt courageously into the unknown.

NINE

The sound of gunshots rang out from the ghost town and swept over the surrounding sand dunes. The four pony riders stopped their mounts as the deafening noise assailed them. The lead rider, White Horse, held his skittish pinto in check as the rifle fire continued to wash over them. Every instinct within his lean, tanned frame told him to lead his three followers away from this place of death and misery, yet the hunger of his tribe's people meant that that course of action was not an option. Raven Wing, Spotted Wolf and Red Hawk and he had been entrusted by the last of his people's elders to venture out from the reservation in order to replenish the meagre rations that the Indian agent dished out.

Ignoring the sound of bullets White Horse tapped his moccasins against the sides of his pinto and encouraged the nervous animal forward.

There was a grim determination carved upon his stolid features: a determination born of necessity rather than choice. The four Cheyennes had spent almost ten days moving from the forested mountains into the desert and back again. Now it was time to collect the goods they had hidden in the dry sand and return through the forest to the reservation.

Unlike during their previous visits to the harsh reality of the arid desert, the sound of incessant gunfire informed them that this time they were not alone.

Most men would have turned their mounts and ridden in the opposite direction from where it was obvious that a gun battle was under way, yet the Cheyennes pressed on, towards the sound of gunfire.

White Horse led his three followers among the vast dunes like the expert hunter he had always been in an attempt to avoid any of them being observed. The nearer they rode to where they had buried their stash of furs and game the louder the shots became.

It was obvious to the intrepid White Horse that the men who were waging their own private war were doing it close to where he and his tribesmen had hidden their precious goods.

To reach them they would have to risk their very lives.

His hooded eyes stared at the sand and the tracks left by the bandits. He could see where the horses had been left and noted the imprints of boots. Every mark told White Horse its own story.

He raised his arm silently and turned to face his fellow tribesmen. All too aware that every sound carried on the air White Horse spoke silently with his hands.

Raven Wing gave a firm nod of his head.

Like phantoms they dismounted their small, sturdy ponies and raced up the dune. There was no noise from any of the Cheyennes as they listened and saw the rifle fire deep within the ghost town. White Horse knelt, raised his left arm and pointed to the drifting gunsmoke.

The disturbed sand just below the ridge of the dune told them that this was where the three riflemen had rested between firing their deadly

Winchesters at the two innocent men trapped in the decaying ghost town. Spotted Wolf glanced around at the discarded bullet casings, then he indicated the spot where they had buried their goods, close to the abandoned saloon. His silent words urged the others to ride down and retrieve their bags of game.

White Horse's narrowed eyes looked over the dune. He shook his head at the suggestion. He knew that the sight of four Cheyennes might scare the white men into turning their weapons on their small hunting party.

Gunsmoke rose up into the cloudless sky as the bandits chased their prey the way the Indians themselves had hunted down their own quarry. White Horse turned away from the brutal battle and spoke again with his hands to the others.

Once more Raven Wing pointed across the crumbling buildings to the place where they had left their collection of small game and furs. There was urgency in his eyes. He knew that the starving members of their tribe needed the supplies as soon as possible. White Horse lowered his head as he too considered the situation. He knew that Raven Wing was correct.

The gunmen were between them and their

vital goods. If the bandits were to discover the furs and skinned animals before he and his fellow braves could retrieve them White Horse doubted if he could restrain his three fellow Cheyennes.

There would be a bloodbath.

White Horse knew that getting their hands on their goods presented a problem. Without them they could not secretly return to the reservation.

As White Horse pondered on their situation Red Hawk, the youngest of the hunters, saw something gleaming a little way below them. With the swiftness of a magpie he raced down the dune and dug the gleaming object out of the sand.

The other three made their way down to where Red Hawk stood holding the tiny object in his hand. White Horse leaned over his friend and instantly realized what Red Hawk had found.

It was a saddle buckle, found only on the saddlery used by Mexicans. It was favoured by the bandits who roamed on both sides of the border.

He uttered the word 'bandit' in his native tongue.

A grim resolve filled the faces of all four hunters.

Again Raven Wing urged White Horse to enter the ghost town to get their hidden food and furs.

This time White Horse agreed. The metal buckle told him that there was no time to lose. The bandits who roamed the barren desert were the most unpredictable and ruthless of any whom they had encountered.

They were the sworn enemies of the Cheyenne.

The Cheyennes moved to their ponies, threw themselves up on to the back of their mounts and drove them on between the sand dunes.

With every stride of the sturdy ponies the sound of the bitter shooting grew ever louder in the ears of the four Cheyenne braves.

This time they did not shy away from the noise of the venomous rifles.

Like ancient knights they valiantly rode without fear through the sandy labyrinth towards the very heart of the ghost town. Whatever fate awaited them the hunting party would face it for the sake of the tribesmen back on the reservation.

There were starving men, women and children who were relying upon the four hunters.

White Horse waved his arm and the hunting party rode on. He was determined not to betray his people's trust.

TEN

Ty Morrow had been lucky when he leapt blindly from the top of the flat rooftop. He had landed squarely on top of a pile of hay bales and then tumbled head over heels until the remnants of an old prairie schooner had stopped him. As he lay winded on his back he could hear that the firing of Winchesters had been momentarily replaced by the sound of approaching spurs. Still dazed, the young drifter scrambled to his feet, filled his lungs with air and started to run back in the direction of the deserted hotel, where he had left his seriously wounded pal.

Yet even though every fibre of his long lean frame seemed to be screaming out in agony after the desperate leap Morrow still knew that he dared not lead the bandits back to where the defenceless Shane waited.

The shots resumed a few moments after Morrow had crashed on to the stacked bales. Even before he clambered back on to his feet he saw the red glowing traces of rifle fire tear through the sky above him.

Morrow reached what was left of a picket fence as the three riflemen appeared at the rear of the flat-roofed building. As he paused by the broken fence to catch his breath all three of the bandits fired their rifles. The fence suddenly disintegrated all around him. Fragments of lumber flew in all directions as the rifle bullets tore through the already crumbling poles.

Morrow fanned the hammer of his gun at them. As they ducked his bullets he made another dash back towards the wide street.

Yet even before he disappeared into the alleyway they started firing again. Bullets barely missed him as he ran for all he was worth back across the expanse of sand towards the Mexicans' three tethered mounts. As Morrow swerved to his right, so that the bandits would not have a clear target at which to aim their lethal rifles, he saw a small building set close to the old hotel that he and Shane had entered just after they had been fired upon.

He was panting like an ancient hound as he kept forcing his aching body to keep moving. He sucked in the dry air and tried to fill his lungs as Cruz and his two lethal cohorts reached the alley and blasted their rifles along its length. The bullets tore across the street and hit a building to his left with incredible force. Huge holes were punched into its decaying fabric.

Morrow knew that the shooters could not have been able to see him or he would already be dead.

An ice-cold chill traced his entire body.

He forced himself to keep running. There was no other choice apart from dying, and Morrow did not want to die.

They were still intent on killing him, he thought. He cocked and fired his gun at the alley and watched as his bullets ripped large sections of the walls apart.

For a brief moment the bandits paused.

Morrow used every precious second of the time he had bought himself and stared at the building directly in his path. The words upon its long board were faded but they seemed to spell 'hardware'.

Like a fox cornered by a pack of ravenous hounds, he ran towards it. He heard large spurs ringing out. Cruz and his cohorts had nearly reached the main street again.

Morrow had to find sanctuary fast.

He kept moving towards the hardware store as rifle bullets cut out from the alleyway.

He raced up on to the boardwalk. With the sound of shooting growing louder Morrow lowered his head and charged at the dilapidated building.

He jumped at what was left of its window. The last of its glass panes shattered and its rotten wooden crossbar splintered into dust as he landed inside the store. He crashed into a barrel and felt his momentum carry him up and over it.

Then he crashed on to the floor.

Dust rose all around him. Morrow stared over the top of the barrel and out through the window. He had a perfect view of the sun-drenched street.

The bandits emerged from between two buildings, still clutching the rifles in their hands. Morrow could see the brilliant sunlight flash along the telescopic sights of Pancho Cruz's weapon. He felt his heart pounding inside his chest as he watched the three bandits continue to search for him.

It was the first time Morrow had been able to study his attackers in detail, and what he saw did nothing but drain his confidence. They looked exactly as he had always imagined ruthless killers would look. There was nothing romantic about the three men as they fanned out and moved across the sandy street in search of him.

Cruz and his followers wore dark, greasy clothing which appeared to have a thousand miles of death clinging to the fabric. They were far more than just dirty, he thought. These men wore clothes that shone. Morrow tried to swallow but it was impossible.

He felt as though he had a rope around his neck.

This was not how it was written up in the dime novels he had grown up reading. These were not men whom he watched, he thought. These were stinking killers. A breed of creature he was unfamiliar with.

His heart raced.

They were obviously so used to killing that it

104

had become second nature to them. They killed people the way normal folks swatted flies, he thought.

Morrow edged up to a kneeling position but remained crouched behind the barrel. He watched the men as they continued to hunt him down as if he were no more than a trophy.

He knew he could not remain where he was. It would not take them long to discover the broken window and put two and two together.

He had to move.

Morrow looked all around the small hardware store and then crawled across the floor towards a side door that he had noticed between a rusted tin bath and coils of ropes. He did not rise until he reached the door. For a fraction of a heartbeat he was relieved, thinking that he had found a way out of the small store.

The feeling would not last long.

As his gloved hands gripped the door handle he found it would not turn. He summoned all his strength and tried to force the handle to turn but it was completely corroded and refused to obey. Years of neglect held it firmly to its warped frame.

'Damn it all!' Morrow cursed. He released his

grip, swung round and rested next to the tin bath, which hung from a hook. His eyes darted to the window. He could see the bandits getting closer.

There had to be another escape route.

But was there?

Was he going to be trapped here? he wondered. Trapped here and blasted into the next world by the stinking dregs that had already wounded Shane and were determined to add him to their gruesome tally.

Morrow rubbed his dry mouth along his shirtsleeve and stared at the gun in his hand. He had no idea how many shots he had fired in his desperate attempt to escape from the bandits. He opened the chamber of his weapon and gazed at the smoking cylinder. Every bullet had been fired, leaving only the spent casings. He carefully shook the casings into the palm of his gloved hand and placed them on top of a box. He pulled fresh bullets from his gunbelt and slid them into the vacant chambers. He swallowed as he heard the noise of the jangling spurs ringing out like tolling bells.

They were on the boardwalk, he thought.

Morrow ducked and stared out through the

veil of cobwebs at the deadly trio.

How could anyone be so unafraid? he wondered. They despised death and challenged it. He shook his head sadly, like a man who knew his time was nearly up.

Then, behind a high pile of boxes at the rear of the room, he spied the edge of another doorframe. He rammed his gun into his holster and climbed over everything between him and the boxes before he managed to get his hands on the door.

It seemed to take every particle of his dwindling strength just to prise the boxes away from the door that they were stacked against, but he did it.

The door was unlocked. He pushed it away from him and forced his lean body through the narrow gap. Without even realizing it Morrow closed the door behind him.

To his surprise he had not emerged into the open air, but was in a dark room. It was so dark that he could not see anything for several moments until his eyes adjusted to the darkness.

It was a storeroom.

There were no windows.

Morrow moved cautiously across it. His boots

kept catching against unseen objects on the floor, but he kept walking until he reached the end wall.

In all his days he had never been anywhere as black as this small room. As his hands rested on the wall he heard the sound of the three bandits entering the store.

He swung around and drew his gun again. Morrow aimed it at the door that he had just come in by and prayed that they would not see the well-hidden entrance into this dark place, as he had done.

The sound of their spurs was like a haunting melody. They moved around the abandoned storeroom just as he had done. He heard one of them trying to force the side door and failing, just as he had failed.

Their voices were raised and sounded angry, but Morrow did not understand a word of what they were saying. All he knew for certain was that they were speaking Spanish.

Then as noisily as they had entered the store they departed. He holstered his gun.

Morrow exhaled and shook his head.

There was a sliver of light in the storeroom. It was as thin as a strand of hair and it traced across the floor right to his boots. Morrow was curious and followed the faint line of illumination to the black wall.

Morrow pulled out a box of matches and struck one.

Its flame rose and then calmed down but the flare had been enough for him to see the very thing he had prayed he would see. He blew the match flame out and tossed it over his shoulder. The match had shown him another door.

His hands groped the well-secured door. During the brief life of the match he had seen a plank of wood preventing the door from being opened by anyone outside who tried to gain entrance.

Morrow lifted the wood and rested it against the wall. His hands searched for the lock and his fingers did not fail him. He found and turned a large key. Like all rusted locks it made a grinding noise as its tumbler was released.

Morrow pulled the door towards him.

A beam of blinding sunlight dazzled him and made him momentarily stop in his tracks. As he raised his hand to shield his eyes a deafening shot rang out.

A huge lump of the door's frame was blasted

from the wall. It narrowly missed Morrow as it bounced back on to him. Startled, Morrow drew his gun and fired a reply. Using his own gunsmoke as cover he ran down to the rear of the building. He had only just turned the corner when another deafening bullet smashed into the wall beside him.

Morrow could hear the spurs of the bandits behind him. He reached around the smouldering corner of the wall and blasted another reply. Then he took to his heels and ran.

He had started down another alley when he saw an overhang above him. Without even thinking he holstered his gun and leapt upwards. His gloved hands gripped the wood and he used his boots to gain purchase on the wall as he clambered up it on to the overhang.

He lay on his belly as the three bandits ran along the alley, then carried on further along the street. He got back to his feet and faced the steep roof.

Morrow scrambled up the wooden shingles and down the other side. When he reached the very edge of the building he jumped down on to a mound of sand.

His mind raced.

He wondered for how long could he elude the bandits?

Pancho Cruz and his vermin had gone to the right, he told himself. He looked to the left to where the three bandits' horses were tethered beside the trough.

He moved through the merciless sun to the horses and pulled the reins free. He then lifted his gun above his head and fired. The sound and the bright flash spooked the horses; they reared up and bolted.

Morrow then dashed into the hotel. It was like visiting an old friend. It was where he and Shane had investigated earlier.

The interior of the building was far cooler now. It felt good to the red-faced youngster as he made his way through to the staircase.

The beginnings of a plan were starting to hatch in his tired mind as he reached the staircase. He cautiously climbed up it and listened to the treads creaking under his weight just as they had done the last time he had ascended them.

Dust fell from the ceiling above him but Morrow continued upwards until he reached the landing. He paused and looked down at the termite-ridden floor between himself and the room he had entered earlier. The boards had provided a feast for the industrious insects for years, he thought as he navigated a safe route into one of the rooms.

As he stood in the doorframe he glanced back at the rickety landing and sighed.

Just like before his boot heels punched holes in the dry boards from the top of the staircase to the doorway. He had successfully made it to the room without breaking his neck, he thought with relief.

Morrow walked carefully across to the window. What was left of its frame was easily pulled away from the wall.

He looked out and surveyed his options. It was a mere five feet to the next building from the window. All he had to do was jump and pray for divine help.

Then he caught sight of the Mexicans as they raced up to the trough. His shot had achieved two things. It had run off their mounts and it had drawn the bandits into his trap. He rested a hip on the sill and watched them as they ranted at one another.

By the sound of it they were mighty angry with him.

Morrow grinned.

They had scared his and Shane's horses off and now he had done the same to theirs.

There ain't much time, he told himself, and he started to pull the spent bullets and throw them across the room. Then he started to reload his six-shooter.

He knew the bandits would follow him into the hotel. That was what he was relying upon. They were carrying so much ammunition on the belts across their chests that the fragile floor would be put under considerable strain.

All he had to do was bide his time and pray.

As he slid bullets into the still warm chambers of his .45 he thought about the advice Shane had given him.

Shoot and run.

Morrow smiled. So far he had managed to follow the instructions.

Suddenly the sound of spurs drifted up into the room where Morrow waited. He swung one leg out of the window and listened to the bandits walking below him.

'We know you are in here, gringo,' Lopez called out as he and the others moved like vermin through the old hotel. 'We are very angry with you. You should not have frightened our horses away. For this we shall kill you, *amigo*.'

Morrow gritted his teeth.

'This gringo ain't afraid of you,' he taunted.

'You should be afraid, *señor*,' Cruz bellowed out. 'You have made me very angry.'

'My heart bleeds for you,' Morrow shouted back.

'It will not be the only thing that bleeds when we get our hands on you, *amigo*,' Cruz returned. 'Normally we would just kill you, but you have to die slowly.'

'Suits me just fine,' Morrow called out.

Pancho Cruz and the others had worked out exactly where the defiant Morrow was hiding. Stealthily they closed in on the staircase and stared up at the landing.

'You shall learn that it does not pay to anger us, *amigo*,' Cruz snarled.

Morrow closed his gun and cocked its hammer, rested a hip on the windowsill and anxiously waited.

'We are coming to get you,' Lopez called, and he laughed loudly from down in the belly of the hotel.

'When we kill you we will find your wounded

amigo and kill him too,' Sanchez added.

Morrow listened to the sound of their spurs, then he heard them crank the mechanism of their rifles. The sound of spent casings bouncing on the floor echoed throughout the hotel.

'I'm up here, you stinking bastards,' Morrow yelled out at the top of his voice. 'Come on up and get me if you got the guts.'

The footsteps seemed to be getting nearer.

'When we find your *amigo* we will torture him for a very long time,' Pancho Cruz growled as he and his two followers reached the foot of the staircase.

Morrow lowered his head, held his gun in his hand and stared at the wide-open door of the room in which he waited.

'They say that the smallest dogs bark the loudest,' he shouted. 'Come on up, you back-shooting Chihuahuas. If you got the guts.'

ELEVEN

The carefully aimed words from Morrow found their target just as he had planned. The bandits gave out a terrifying whoop which would have made even the bravest of souls doubt the sanity of riling them. Juan Sanchez gripped his Winchester in both hands and ran up the staircase with Cruz and Lopez close on his heels. Morrow was braced halfway out of the window. The sight of Sanchez as he appeared at the top of the staircase was frightening. Morrow saw the rifle turn in his direction. He blasted his .45 wildly.

The bandit was neither afraid nor deterred. He pulled on the trigger of his rifle and sent a blistering shot towards Morrow. The bullet skimmed the shoulder of the youngster as he somehow managed to fire another shot back at the bandit.

Sanchez glared with bloodshot eyes at Morrow perched on the windowsill. A twisted smile stretched across his filthy features as the Mexican cocked his Winchester and strode forward. Suddenly the floor beneath his boots gave way. There was an unholy rending sound which stopped both Lopez and Cruz in their tracks upon the staircase.

Only one man realized what was happening. Morrow clung to the window frame and watched a mighty cloud of dust erupt around Sanchez as the floor beneath him gave way.

There was a horrific noise as the entire landing collapsed under the weight of the startled bandit. Morrow watched Sanchez disappear from view as gravity sucked him down into the abyss.

Yet even as Sanchez was falling he still managed to squeeze the trigger of his rifle one last time before being engulfed in the decaying wreckage.

Morrow eased the rest of his body out of the window frame and balanced himself. Through the clouds of choking dust that continued to spew up from the chasm he watched Cruz and Lopez reach the top of the staircase. Morrow fired into the swirling dust at the bandits. He did not wait to see the outcome of his shot. They ducked and that was long enough for Morrow to swing out from the window and jump the five feet separating the two buildings.

Somehow through luck rather than skill he landed on the adjacent roof. Like so many of the other buildings in the ghost town the roof was brittle. Morrow felt part of the roof give way under the impact, but he grabbed hold of a metal chimney stack before he fell.

As Morrow steadied himself he heard and saw a volley of bullets rip through the window frame from where he had just jumped.

'Reckon I sure stomped on their corns,' he told himself as he ran down the roof slope. He jumped on to the building's veranda, clambered over the safety rail and dropped down to the ground.

Morrow knew there was no way either of the remaining bandits could reach the hotel room from where he had just leapt. If they wanted to catch him they would have to retrace their tracks and return to the street.

He stood, swung full circle and then saw a few buildings further up the street. Morrow ran towards them.

The choking was dust still filling the entire hotel as Cruz and Lopez descended back to the ground floor. Both the bandits climbed over piles of debris in search of Sanchez. They feverishly clawed away at rubble, chunks of plaster and a mass of splintered wood until their hands came upon gore.

Through the dust they stared down at the bloody bandit. A long broken wooden support had driven its way straight through the now lifeless outlaw. What was left of Sanchez looked more like a ghost than anything either of them had ever seen. They crossed themselves fearfully.

The body was covered in white plaster dust. The unmistakable red stain had already spread through the white powder from where the wooden staff had skewered Sanchez.

Lopez leaned over his fellow bandit, then looked at Pancho Cruz. They had done many things to their defenceless victims over the years, but nothing to compare with this.

'I think he is dead, Pancho,' Lopez said in

total shock.

'*Sí*, I think you are right, Francisco.' Pancho Cruz leaned over and pulled the Winchester from the rigid death-grip of the bandit. He tucked it under his arm and began to clamber back towards the safer section of the hotel.

Lopez trailed Cruz. 'I do not like this town. It is dangerous,' he complained.

Cruz lifted his own rifle and snarled. 'The gringo thinks he is very clever but he shall soon discover that it does not pay to anger Pancho Cruz. Come, Francisco.'

The bandits left their fallen cohort beneath the rubble and hurried back into the street. As Lopez neared the hitching rail he scratched his chin.

'How are we going to leave here without our horses, Pancho?' he asked.

'They will return when they remember the water in the trough, *amigo*,' Cruz said. He peered along the street. For a brief moment he caught a glimpse of Morrow shouldering his way into a boarded-up gun store. 'First we have to kill that gringo.'

TWELVE

The Cheyennes suddenly emerged from between two of the towering dunes and drove their unshod ponies through the crumbling structures on towards the place where they had concealed their own treasure. Unlike the two bandits at the other end of the long winding thoroughfare, they were not seeking gold and silver coins. The treasure they sought was far more valuable to them and their people.

They rode like phantoms through the shimmering heat to where they had hidden the bulk of their hunting bag. The four braves did not stay out in the open for long. They drove their ponies straight to where they had buried their precious goods, between two buildings.

White Horse remained atop his pony and placed an arrow on the drawstring of his bow. He stood guard at the end of the alley as his three fellow Cheyennes dismounted and started to dig with their hands.

Red Hawk pulled a wad of rawhide leather laces from his belt as they dragged the furs and freshly killed game from the sandpit. As the small animals were laid on top of one of the larger pelts he expertly tied them in manageable bundles.

White Horse remained alert and watched the two Mexican bandits as they approached. There was still 300 yards between the feverishly working braves and the two men with an arsenal of weaponry and ammunition.

Pancho Cruz and Francisco Lopez had noticed the unexpected arrival of the four Cheyennes before they had started to walk down the middle of the wide street but neither man was concerned. The braves had brought them the gift of horseflesh.

First, though, they had to find and kill the defiant gringo who had lured them into a trap.

A trap which had cost one of them his life.

'I see one of the Injuns poking his nose out of

the alleyway, *amigo*,' Lopez remarked as he walked beside Cruz. 'He has got a bow and arrow.'

Cruz grunted with derision. 'They are like children, Francisco. They use toys against men with real weapons. We shall kill them all after we have found the gringo.'

They stopped and turned towards the gun store. The shadows of their unsavoury forms spread across the sand as they looked at the broken door.

'That is the place the gringo forced his worthless carcass into, Francisco,' Cruz said. He swiftly pushed the hand guard down on his rifle, then brought it up again.

'Where has he gone, Pancho?' Lopez wondered as they approached the store, then poked the barrels of their rifles into it.

Cruz looked up at the second floor. 'I think he is trying to set another trap, *amigo*.'

Lopez kept glancing over his shoulder at the distant but unmistakable Cheyenne warrior, who was observing their every move.

'The gringo is very clever, Pancho,' Lopez said. 'He makes traps and they are deadly.'

Pancho Cruz pulled a rusted old lantern off

the wall beside the broken door and shook it beside his ear. It still had coal-tar oil in its bowl. He turned the lantern upside down for a brief moment, just for long enough to soak its wick in the inflammable liquid.

'What are you doing, Pancho?' Lopez asked. 'It is not dark inside the store. We do not need a lantern.'

Pancho Cruz glanced up at the window above them and smiled. He struck a match and touched the lantern's wick. The entire lantern was soon engulfed in flame. Cruz held it with his gloved hand and stared at it.

'We are not seeking the gringo, Francisco,' Cruz said. 'The fire shall look for him instead.'

Cruz tossed the lantern into the gun store, then backed away. In seconds the entire tinder-dry store had become an inferno. Scarlet flames erupted from every window as the fire rapidly began to consume the building. Black smoke billowed out into the street from the cracks and gaps in the broken walls.

Lopez started to laugh.

'You are very clever, *amigo*.'

Cruz gave a firm nod of his head and spat at the burning building. 'Burn, gringo. Burn.'

As the all-consuming blaze sent smoke and flame high into the blue sky a shot rang out. It tore the sombrero from Lopez's head. Both bandits dropped on to one knee and aimed their Winchesters down the long street.

'The Injun shot at us, Pancho,' Lopez shouted in fright, staring wide-eyed at White Horse.

Cruz narrowed his eyes. 'It was not the Cheyenne, Francisco. He has only a bow and arrow in his hands.'

Lopez plucked his large sombrero off the sand and stared at the bullet hole in its crown. 'If it was not the Injun who was it?'

Cruz rose back to his full height and surveyed the town. Both bandits kept their rifles primed and ready.

'The shot came from all the way down there.' Cruz pointed.

Lopez looked bewildered as he placed his hat upon his head. 'But the gringo could not have run that far away in such a short time, Pancho. Even if he had escaped he could not have got there so soon.'

Cruz led his cohort across the sand as shadows from the black smoke danced across the surface of the ground. The two bandits reached a far wall and rested against it.

'You are right, Francisco. It could not have been the gringo.' Cruz was thoughtful. 'The Cheyenne did not shoot a gun either.'

'Then who shot at us, *amigo*?'

Pancho Cruz narrowed his eyes. His gaze darted from one place to another until he spotted the man who had fired a shot at them. Cruz raised his rifle and jabbed at the air.

'He did.' He pointed to the veranda and the frail figure of Clint Shane standing upon it.

Cruz lifted his rifle and eased its stock into his shoulder. He adjusted the telescopic sight until he had the blood-soaked figure in the cross-hairs.

'Now it is time for the other gringo to die,' Cruz said.

THIRTEEN

Morrow had barely escaped the flames that suddenly engulfed the gun store by throwing himself out of a rear window. Then he crawled beneath the burning building towards the main street. He could feel the heat from the raging inferno on his back as he emerged into the sunlight and slid behind a trough set directly opposite the door of the gun store. His clothes smoked as he crawled behind the trough and stared at what was left of the crumbling building.

The heat from the rampaging blaze was too hot for Morrow as he crouched beside the trough. Even more than fifteen feet from the burning building he could feel his skin blistering. Morrow rose up on to his knees and saw Pancho Cruz staring through his gun sights towards the old hotel.

Morrow rubbed his eyes and saw that the target was Shane, who had somehow ventured out on to the veranda.

The young drifter jumped to his feet and drew his six-shooter from its holster. He fanned his hammer and saw his bullets tear into the wooden wall behind the two bandits.

Cruz and Lopez ducked as splinters of wood rained over them. They swung around just as the building behind Morrow collapsed into a fiery heap. A huge mushroom-shaped black cloud rose into the air behind him. Millions of cinders floated on the turbulent air and landed on the buildings to either side of it.

Within seconds flames started to rise from them as well.

Morrow saw the sun reflect off the telescopic sight as Cruz trained his rifle upon him. He ran and jumped behind another empty trough as rifle bullets came sizzling through the smoke-filled air and into the wooden building.

The bullets went straight through the trough and blasted the back off it.

Panic stricken, Morrow knew that none of the wooden objects in the ghost town were sturdy enough to withstand bullets. Ever since they had first been constructed the sun had mercilessly sucked every ounce of moisture from the wooden buildings, leaving most of them brittle.

He crawled towards the nearest building. Even though it too was now alight he rose and kicked its door off its hinges and entered. Morrow had no sooner paused than a dozen shots followed him in. Bullets cut all around his lean frame and shattered a glass display case on the far wall. Morrow dived to one side and looked through the black smoke.

Both of the bandits were striding towards him with vengeance burning inside their malodorous bodies. They cranked their rifles again, sending spent casings flying. They were coming. Coming to finish him off.

Knowing there was no time to lose, Morrow leapt over the broken glass and raced to the rear door.

At least he had taken their minds off Shane, he thought. He raised his leg and kicked out at the rear door. It shattered into matchwood.

The stench of burning was everywhere. The sound of wood exploding as it was engulfed by the spreading fire was all that filled his ears. Smoke in the rear alley made it impossible to see anything clearly, especially any safe route away from the two deadly bandits.

Morrow glanced back as the bandits entered the store and blasted their rifles at him. His flesh felt the heat of their bullets as he turned and raced further away from the smouldering ashes.

Cruz and Lopez gave chase. They had never been so close to their prey before. Now as they raced into the choking clouds of black smoke they knew it was only a matter of time before they would find their target.

Less than 200 yards away from the billowing smoke, Shane staggered aimlessly along the hotel veranda. His shirt was drenched in blood as he reached a flight of wooden steps and tried to make his way down them. He knew something was wrong but his delirious mind was playing tricks on him.

Nothing was as it seemed.

Shane's entire world was a blur.

Fever was now controlling the youngster's

actions. He no longer had any idea of what he was doing. He did not know why he was out on the veranda, but vaguely remembered shooting at the men in large hats.

But even that was not a memory he trusted.

His only thought was for his friend.

Like a drunkard he descended the steps with his gun in his left hand. When he reached the ground a cloud as dense as the one that hung over the burning buildings enveloped his confused mind.

Suddenly he was trapped in a whirlpool. His head was spinning like a child's top. He tried to stop himself from falling into the whirlpool, but it was useless.

Shane toppled.

He kept falling. He was helpless to stop. Wherever he was going he knew it was somewhere he had never been before. He hit the ground hard.

White Horse watched as his fellow braves secured the last of their goods on to the backs of their ponies and mounted. He then turned his own pinto and heeled the small horse to walk out of the alley.

131

There was no sign of the sombrero-wearing bandits.

He waved his braves forward. Red Hawk, Spotted Wolf and Raven Wing galloped along the wide street and disappeared into the dunes.

White Horse was about to drive his own pony in pursuit of his fellow Cheyennes when he saw Clint Shane collapse at the foot of the hotel steps.

Every instinct told him to ignore the pitiful young drifter and follow his fellow braves back into the safety of the dunes. His people had never known anything but trouble from white men, who now lived off the fruits of his old ancestral lands.

A generation of broken promises and violated treaties still could not stop White Horse from riding to where Shane lay in a bloody heap.

He pulled back on his rope reins, looped his leg over the white mane of his pinto, dropped to the ground and knelt beside the wounded Shane. He turned the bloodstained figure over and stared at the severe injuries Shane had suffered. He had seen many similar wounds over the years.

Without hesitating White Horse pulled a long

132

slim dagger from his beaded belt and tore
Shane's shirt apart. He narrowed his eyes and
pushed the pointed tip of the knife into the
unconscious man's flesh.

FOURTEEN

Ezra Blake raised his arm and pulled back on his long leathers. His mount stopped as Sergeant Riley reined in beside him and the rest of the small troop brought their horses to an abrupt halt. Dust continued to flow into the shimmering heat haze as Blake stood in his stirrups and stared ahead at the ghost town. Then he sat back down and looked at the burly Riley.

'Holy smoke, Riley,' he exclaimed. 'It sounds as though someone's waging a war out there.'

Riley leaned over the neck of his lathered-up mount. 'I reckon you're right, Captain. It sounds as if it's coming from that abandoned town yonder.'

Blake rubbed his gauntlet across his face. 'I bet

it's those damn Cheyennes. They've done exactly what I feared they'd do. They're attacking settlers.'

The seasoned sergeant moved his mount closer to his superior officer and whispered.

'There ain't no settlers within a hundred miles of here, Captain,' Riley told him. 'And that ain't old Henrys being fired. That's Winchesters. Winchesters and handguns. The Cheyennes ain't got either.'

Like so many cut from his cloth Captain Blake did not like to be contradicted. He glared at the sergeant.

'I said it was the Cheyennes, Riley. We're chasing four renegade Cheyennes who have fled the reservation. It's my opinion they have started to run amok.'

Riley sighed heavily and stared at the young officer in dismay. 'No offence, but I've been riding this territory for the longest while and I'm certain that those Injuns are simply out hunting. They'd not have let a white man even see them, let alone fight them.'

Blake screwed up his eyes and stared at the stalwart Riley. He pointed a gloved finger and growled.

'Eyewash. If I say it's the Cheyenne that's doing the shooting then that's exactly who's doing the shooting, Riley. Do you understand me?'

The man with three golden chevrons on his sleeves gave a reluctant nod of his head.

'Yes, sir,' he croaked. 'I understand.'

'Good.' Blake turned to the rest of his troop. 'Are you ready to kick some feather-heads, men?'

The mounted men shouted their agreement as with one voice. Like their newly commissioned officer they were also new to the territory.

Captain Blake turned back on his saddle, pulled the brim of his hat down to shield his eyes from the glare of the sun and adjusted his sabre.

'It does not pay in this army to disagree with a superior officer, Riley,' he said from the corner of his mouth. 'Not unless you want to end up back in the ranks. Do you want to lose those stripes?'

Riley shook his head. 'No, sir. I don't.'

Blake smiled and gathered his reins in his hands.

'I'm pleased that you've finally seen sense. Now we shall go and stop those Cheyennes from slaughtering any more innocents,' he said. 'If the savages don't like it then we shall bury the savages.'

Riley looked at Blake's profile.

'Bury them?' he questioned.

Blake stared at Riley. 'Exactly. That's how men climb through the ranks in this army, Sergeant. Ask George Custer if you think I'm wrong.'

'I reckon you're right, sir.'

'I'm always right,' Blake snapped. 'Now, in your expert opinion, how far do you think it is to that town?'

'About two miles,' Riley replied.

'Forward ho!' Blake drew his sabre and waved his troop on. The cavalry charged through the desert towards the ghost town at breakneck pace There was an urgency in Blake's spurs. It was not shared by Sergeant Riley.

FIFTEEN

The two bandits strode from the choking smoke of the burning buildings and started to home in on their prey. They were like demonic monsters that had been created in the bowels of Hell as they slowly trailed their victim's tracks. Beads of sweat tracked down from their sombreros across their greasy features. The menacing sound of their spurs rang out with every step they took.

Their shadows were lengthening as the afternoon sun began its inevitable descent. Pancho Cruz and Francisco Lopez moved through the blinding smoke and cinders towards the derelict saloon with their prized Winchesters held at hip height. Their narrowed eyes studied the soft sand as they trailed the boot marks left by the fleeing Morrow towards the abandoned saloon.

They neither spoke nor blinked as they approached the dilapidated building with their primed weaponry ready for action.

They were on an unholy mission.

They were about to kill Morrow and could actually taste his desperate scent in the air. They were like ravenous dogs hunting down their unwary prey. Only his death would satisfy them now.

The grim sound of crashing timbers as they burned, blackened and fell into the smouldering heaps of ashes resounded throughout the ghost town, a gruesome portent of impending death.

The bandits reached the saloon. They studied it coldly. Cruz stepped up on to the boardwalk and strode towards the outer door. It was slightly ajar as he signalled to Lopez to move to the other side of the saloon's entrance.

They were angry now.

Angrier than they had ever been.

The young Morrow had mocked them. He had also lured them into a trap, which had caused one of them to lose his life. Neither of the bandits seemed willing to let this go unavenged.

It was as though their very manhood had been challenged.

139

Morrow had to die. It was as simple as that.

Even though the bandits knew that their hunt was delaying them from digging up and retrieving their hidden loot, they were willing to spend the time.

They would not be satisfied until they had the head of Morrow as a trophy.

Cruz rubbed his shoulder along the wall and stared in through the gap left by the unclosed door. The swing doors were clearly visible just inside the large outer ones. His eyes darted to those of his deadly companion and instructed the bandit to do as he did.

After years of riding together each bandit seemed to know exactly what the other was thinking. At precisely the same moment both Cruz and Lopez dragged the outer doors apart and rushed through the saloon's swing doors into the dark interior with their rifles blazing.

They unleashed a dozen shots before pausing. The sheer noise from their weapons seemed to shake the weakened walls. Dust fell from the ceiling like snow as the two ruthless bandits stopped in their tracks.

Gunsmoke filled the room as Cruz stared down at the whiskey bottle on a table that stood close to the doors. He lifted it to his lips and took a mouthful of the powerful liquor.

'The gringo was here, *amigo*,' he stated. He lowered the bottle and placed it back on to the dust-covered table.

Lopez walked deeper into the saloon and investigated every possible hiding-place.

'He is not here any longer, Pancho,' he said, and spat.

Cruz trailed his cohort into the middle of the saloon and looked around them. The evidence of Morrow's and Shane's first visit to the abandoned saloon was everywhere.

The outlaw looked at the marks in the dust and gave a slow, knowing nod. He then saw the fresher trail left by Morrow only moments earlier. They led to the side door.

'The gringo rushed through here, Francisco.' Cruz pointed at the tracks left by the racing Morrow. 'He is very scared.'

Lopez laughed. 'He is not so stupid, I think.'

Cruz paused and thought for a moment. The cunning bandit cocked his rifle again. A spent bullet casing bounced across the floor.

'He has gone to his *amigo*, Francisco,' Cruz said. 'The one who shot at us from the hotel veranda.'

141

Lopez nodded. 'I think you might be right.'

'The gringos are just delaying their deaths,' Cruz said coldly, cradling his rifle. 'But death will not be cheated.'

Cruz paced across the floor, back to the swing doors and stared over them out into the sun-baked street. The clouds of black smoke were getting thicker as more tinder-dry buildings were consumed by the now out-of-control fire. The bandit pushed the doors apart and stepped out on to the boardwalk.

Lopez followed. 'The fire is very bad.'

Cruz stepped to the edge of the boardwalk and glanced along the street to where Shane had fired his shot from. The young drifter was no longer in sight. Cruz then turned and looked back to where he had thrown the lantern. His eyes narrowed as he stared in disbelief at the raging inferno he had created. There were now at least three of the rickety buildings totally ablaze.

'You are right, Francisco. It is bad,' he agreed. He lowered the barrel of the rifle and stared at the fast-moving fire. It was travelling more rapidly along the street than he would have imagined possible.

'Soon the flames will be eating our money, *amigo*,' Lopez said fearfully. 'I do not like that. Half of our treasure is paper money, Pancho.'

The words of his cohort chilled Cruz. A sudden desperation filled his blackened heart. Lopez was correct. Half of their loot *was* paper money.

'Quick, Francisco,' Cruz urged. 'We must get to our treasure before the fire does.'

From the corner of the street Ty Morrow watched as the two bandits suddenly took flight and raced towards the fire. He could not understand why they were so totally frantic.

Seeing the pair dash into a smoke-filled alley close to where the raging inferno was approaching, Morrow ran across the wide expanse of sand to the opposite side of the street.

He leapt up on to the boardwalk, leaned against a wooden upright and glanced at the alley that he had seen the bandits enter. Smoke was now swirling around the street as one building after another fell to the inexorable flames.

His mind raced.

Why were they risking being burned alive? Morrow wondered.

They could not be following him. He had not gone into that alley in his attempts to elude them.

So why had they entered it?

Then a more important thought filled his mind. As Morrow gripped the upright he recalled seeing Shane up on the hotel veranda. He swung on his heel and stared down through the black smoke to the hotel.

Morrow pushed his hat off his brow.

Shane was no longer there, he thought. Where had he gone?

Morrow knew that, wherever Shane might have gone, his severe wounds would soon kill him. He stepped forward and rubbed his eyes in a vain attempt to see through the cloud of blinding smoke. The acrid stench of burning filled his nostrils and tormented his eyes. He pulled his shirt tail out of his belt and leaned over. He dried his eyes and then looked up again.

'Where in tarnation have you gone, Clint?' he muttered under his breath. 'I got enough trouble with them bandits without worrying about where you are.'

Morrow quickly glanced over his shoulder. He could not see either of the men who were intent on killing him. He could barely see the alley that they had run into any longer, as more and more choking smoke filled the street. Morrow realized that he had to find out what had happened to his friend. He gritted his teeth and started to run towards the hotel.

A shot rang out.

Morrow felt the powerful impact as a bullet caught his two-inch left boot heel. It lifted his trailing leg off the ground.

He cartwheeled like a rag doll and was thrown heavily into a storefront. Morrow tumbled and hit the ground hard. He lay dazed for a few seconds on the boardwalk. He was about to rise when another shot came hurtling from out of the dense cloud of smoke.

The red-hot taper cut through the smoke in search of him.

Morrow ducked and held his hands over his head as two more rifle shots punched holes in the wall above his head.

He blinked hard and saw another flash of red venom tearing through the black smoke. The bullet hit the crooked crossbar of a hitching rail and shattered a window above his head. Fragments of glass fell over him.

145

His mind was racing as he realized that the shots were coming from the direction of the alley. One or both of the bandits were again using him for target practice. Another rifle bullet blasted at him. It carved across his prostrate body, ripping his shirt apart and burning his flesh.

With the agility of a monkey, Morrow scrambled off the boardwalk and dropped down on to the sand. He then rolled behind a dry water trough.

Again a shot rang out and knocked another hole in the storefront. Morrow crawled to the end of the trough and drew his gun. His eyes narrowed and tried to see through the growing cloud of smoke.

Suddenly he realized that whoever was firing at him could see little better than he could. The smoke was shielding them both from one another's deadly weapons.

The sound of the menacing spurs suddenly rang out as the two bandits made their way from the alley.

Then Morrow saw them.

It was their legs that he saw first as they walked from the alley carrying four hefty saddle-bags.

146

Morrow squinted and then heard their distinctive voices.

'Why do you hide, gringo?' Cruz shouted. 'You know that we are going to kill you.'

Morrow heard the words aimed at him. Even the fragmented English that spilled from the bandit's mouth did not diminish the chilling statement. He gripped his gun tightly in his hand and listened to the spurs jangling in the smoke. They were getting closer with every beat of his pounding heart.

Then there was a horrific crashing sound.

Another of the burning buildings collapsed. A million cinders erupted like a swarm of fireflies from the scarlet belly of the flames. What had been a rickety building only minutes before was now little more than a pile of embers, with protruding blackened timbers the only reminder of what it had once been.

It had sounded like a stick of dynamite exploding and the sudden noise had caused both bandits to hunch their shoulders as they anticipated that the building would fall on to them.

That was all the encouragement Morrow needed.

He closed one eye and fired blindly into the

swirling smoke. Then he got up on to his knees, cocked his hammer again and squeezed the trigger.

Morrow had never hit anything he had aimed at with his six-shooter before. It came as a shock when he saw two of the saddle-bags drop to the ground as one of the bandits fell to his knees. Lopez bent forward, clutching his guts. The large sombrero fell on to the sand in front of him as he released his grip on his Winchester and dragged his .45 from its holster.

The bandit blasted six shots at the trough.

Chunks of wood flew in all directions from the corner of the trough as Morrow waited for a brief pause in the firing. When Lopez ran out of ammunition Morrow swung his arm around and blasted at the kneeling bandit.

The Remington flew from Lopez's hand as the bullet hit him. He rocked on his knees, then fell lifelessly into his own gore.

'That was a big mistake, gringo,' Pancho Cruz screamed out. He stared down at his dead cohort in total shock and felt an uncontrollable rage well up inside him. He cocked his rifle and squeezed its trigger as he stood beside the stricken Lopez.

The bullet caught the crown of Morrow's Stetson and tore it from his head. Morrow felt as if he had just had an axe crease his scalp. A trickle of blood ran down his forehead and into his eyes.

As Morrow wiped his sleeve across his face the sound of spurs drew closer. The bandit was walking and firing his rifle at the trough. With each shot more and more of its already bullet-ridden frame was torn away.

Morrow moved hastily to the other end of the trough just in time to see Cruz jumping over the boardwalk and taking refuge in a doorway less than twenty feet from where he was huddled.

Desperately, Morrow fanned his gun hammer until the .45 was empty. Smoke trailed from the barrel of the weapon as the young drifter stared at it.

'Damn it all!' he cursed.

His fingers searched for bullets along his belt. They found nothing but the empty leather loops. Suddenly the sound of laughter washed over him as Cruz walked along the boardwalk towards him.

Then he heard the sound of spurs.

The jangling of the bandit's spurs rang out with every stride that Cruz took. Morrow got on his knees and unbuckled his belt. He spread it out before him and saw two unused shells. He shook the spent casings from his six-shooter and teased the bullets out of the belt.

The sound of the spurs grew louder.

Morrow looked up from fumbling with his bullets.

The sight of the bandit greeted his eyes. It was a sight that filled Morrow with terror. He dropped the bullets and stared at the smiling face of the merciless killer. For the first time in his short life he knew what it was like to look into the face of death.

Death wore a sombrero.

Pancho Cruz was smiling and walking steadily towards him with his Winchester held at hip level. It was aimed directly at Morrow's pounding heart. Cruz stopped ten feet from the terrified Morrow and tilted his head back.

'Get up, gringo,' Cruz hissed like a rattler.

Morrow dropped his gun and rose to his full height.

'I'm up,' he said.

Cruz looked at the young drifter as if in disbelief. It seemed impossible to the hardened bandit that he and his cohorts could have had so much trouble from anyone as young as Morrow.

'Where is your *amigo*?' Cruz asked, pulling the rifle hammer back with his thumb until it locked into position.

'Damned if I know,' Morrow replied honestly.

'Tell me the truth,' Cruz snorted. He placed the heavy saddle-bags down on the boardwalk and sighed. 'If you lie I shall kill you very slowly, *amigo*. Tell me the truth and your death shall be swift.'

Before Morrow could speak again Pancho Cruz was knocked violently backwards by a perfectly placed arrow which flew from over Morrow's shoulder and sank into the bandit's chest. The lethal projectile had found the gap in the ammunition belts hung across Cruz's chest.

There was a look of total bewilderment on Cruz's hardened features. He rocked on his heels as his shaking hands aimed his rifle at Morrow again.

Then another arrow came buzzing from behind Morrow. It caught the bandit in his throat. The Winchester flew into the air as it left Cruz's hands. The bandit somehow managed to remain upright as his icy glare burned into the equally startled Morrow.

Blood spread from the bandit's body as he stumbled, then fell face first into the empty water trough.

Ty Morrow looked down at the body, then swung around and stared along the street. He could not see anyone, but he knew his life had been saved by an expert archer.

Unafraid, Morrow ran through the smoke and did not stop until he reached the hotel. He was about to race up the wooden steps to the veranda when something caught his eye and stopped him in his tracks.

He stared down at the sand at the foot of the steps.

It was covered in blood.

Morrow knelt and touched the sand with his gloved fingers thoughtfully. He looked up and caught a glimpse of movement behind the hotel.

Even though he was unarmed Morrow was strangely unafraid as he strode to where he had seen the fleeting glimpse of movement.

As he turned the corner of the hotel he saw White Horse standing over the unconscious Shane. He held the bow in his hands, an arrow resting upon its taut string.

'Howdy,' Morrow said. His eyes darted

between the Cheyenne and his friend.

The Cheyenne did not utter a word but kept the bow trained upon him. Morrow inhaled a lungful of courage and walked to where his friend lay upon the sand.

He dropped on to his knees and stared at the neat wound on Shane's shoulder. It had been stitched together crudely with catgut. The graze on his friend's head was covered in a salve which Morrow did not recognize.

Morrow looked up at White Horse and smiled.

'Thanks,' he said. 'Clint might not pull through but you tried your best.'

White Horse lowered the bow and showed Morrow a bloody lump of lead which he held in the palm of his hand. Morrow looked at the bullet and nodded.

'You risked your life to cut this out of my pal's shoulder?' Morrow sighed as his fingertips toyed with the lump of bloody lead. White Horse stood silently beside his pony. There was no expression upon his face.

Then the sound of horses suddenly broke the relative silence. Morrow got to his feet and walked back to the corner.

He could see the small troop of cavalrymen

riding through the billowing smoke.

'Soldiers,' he muttered. He wiped more blood from his face and watched the riders surveying the carnage. 'I wonder what they're doing here?'

Morrow turned round and saw White Horse grab the mane of his pinto and throw himself up on to its blanket. Both men stared into one another's eyes.

Nothing was said.

White Horse turned his pony and thundered away.

FINALE

Ty Morrow sat on the sand next to his friend as Shane opened his eyes and looked around. He was confused but no longer felt the constant throbbing of the lead ball in his shoulder. He knew he was better than he had been but wondered how.

'What happened, Ty?' Shane asked.

'A few things,' Morrow answered as two horses appeared from round the corner and hovered above them. 'Nothing to get troubled about.'

Shane screwed up his eyes and stared up at the two soldiers. 'What in tarnation are troopers doing here, Ty? Is this another one of them mixed-up dreams that have been haunting me since I was shot? Are they real, Ty?'

'We're real enough,' Blake said. 'I imagine that the two horses we found out in the dunes must belong to you. My troopers have them for you.'

'Much obliged, Captain.' Morrow nodded.

'Have you seen any Cheyennes?' Blake questioned.

Morrow did not say anything. He just placed a cigarette in the corner of his mouth and struck a match. He inhaled the smoke and pushed the burning matchstick into the sand.

Captain Blake looked down at the two drifters.

'Did Cheyenne hostiles do this?' he asked.

Morrow shook his head. 'Nope. It was them dead Mexican bandits down yonder.'

'Did the Cheyennes kill them and shoot your friend as well?' Blake asked. Riley dismounted and leaned over Shane with a canteen.

'I never seen any Injuns,' Shane said. He accepted Riley's canteen.

'Me neither. I ain't seen any Cheyenne hostiles, Captain,' Morrow said, smoke drifting from his lips. 'What do they look like?'

Blake frowned. 'There happens to be a dead Mexican in a trough down the street with two arrows in him, young man. Are you telling me that you haven't seen any Cheyenne hostiles around here?'

'Yep.' Morrow smiled. 'That's what I'm telling you, Captain.'

Riley glanced at Morrow and grinned. He rose up and screwed the stopper back on his canteen.

'I told you that them Injuns ain't out to kill folks, Captain,' he said.

Blake looked puzzled and also very angry.

'There are two dead bandits in town and one of them was killed with arrows, Sergeant,' he said angrily.

'Three bandits,' Morrow corrected.

'Three?' Blake narrowed his eyes.

'Yep, there's one in the hotel at the far end of town,' Morrow told him.

'You killed them, Ty?' Shane gasped.

'I sure did and I claim the reward money.' Morrow tapped the ash from his cigarette. 'I reckon them bandits are worth a few bucks.'

'*You* killed them?' Blake queried.

'I sure did,' Morrow repeated, raising his eyebrows. 'I fought like a tiger.'

Shane stared at his pal. 'Did you shoot and run like I told you?'

'I sure did, Clint,' Morrow said. 'I never have

done so much running and shooting in all my life.'

Riley patted Morrow on the shoulder. 'You're a fine young man, and no mistake. You remind me of my sister's eldest.'

'Thank you kindly, Sergeant.' Morrow grinned.

'If I might rudely interrupt?' Captain Blake straightened in his saddle and glared down at Morrow. 'Why has one of them bandits got two arrows in him?'

Morrow stood up and beat the sand from his pants.

'Ain't it obvious?' he asked.

Riley looked up at his superior.

'Ain't it obvious, Captain?'

Blake shook his head, looking flustered.

'No. It is anything but obvious to me. Why would you use a bow? You had a gun and shot one of them in the street and then you resorted to a bow and arrow. Why?'

'I ran out of ammunition,' Morrow replied, with a shrug.

'I still say it was the Cheyennes,' Blake insisted. 'Why are you covering for them? Where's the damn bow? Answer me that.'

Morrow thought for a moment.

'The spooks must have stolen it,' he replied wryly.

'Spooks?' Blake repeated. 'What spooks?'

'This is a ghost town, ain't it?' Morrow inhaled on his cigarette. 'Reckon one of them must have made it vanish. This is a mighty scary town.'

'I've heard enough of this gibberish.' Blake turned his mount. 'Come on, Riley. This man is loco.'

Morrow watched as Riley mounted his horse and followed the captain back towards the rest of their troopers. He dropped the cigarette and crushed it under his broken heel. Shane stared up at him.

'There's something you ain't telling me, Ty,' he said.

Morrow grinned.

'There's quite a lot, Clint,' he admitted.

'Who cut the lead out of my shoulder?' Shane asked. 'Was it a Cheyenne by any chance?'

Morrow shrugged.

'I'll tell you the whole story when them soldier boys have left town, Clint,' he said.

Shane propped himself up and looked hard at his pal.

'What happened to the bow?' he wondered.

159

'How does a bandit get killed by two arrows when there ain't a bow anyplace?'

Morrow rested his knuckles on his hips and stared down at his pal. There was no way he was going to betray White Horse before the Indian had a chance to escape.

'Have you ever heard about a varmint named Cupid?'

'Eyewash.' Shane sighed.

'Nope, I'm sure his name was Cupid, Clint.' Morrow smiled broadly and then touched his lips. 'Don't tell anyone but I think he might have been a Cheyenne.'